BURIED ALIVE!

Slocum saw the flare of a length of black miner's fuse being lit.

He pounded forward, trying to get out of the mine. Never had he run faster—but to no avail.

The explosion picked him up and tossed him back into the mine. Dust billowed and choked him, and he no longer saw the bright opening filled with spring. He was trapped in the mine!

DON'T MISS THESE
ALL-ACTION WESTERN SERIES
FROM THE BERKLEY PUBLISHING GROUP

THE GUNSMITH by J. R. Roberts
Clint Adams was a legend among lawmen, outlaws, and ladies. They called him . . . the Gunsmith.

LONGARM by Tabor Evans
The popular long-running series about U.S. Deputy Marshal Long—his life, his loves, his fight for justice.

LONE STAR by Wesley Ellis
The blazing adventures of Jessica Starbuck and the martial arts master, Ki. Over eight million copies in print.

SLOCUM by Jake Logan
Today's longest-running action Western. John Slocum rides a deadly trail of hot blood and cold steel.

JAKE LOGAN

SLOCUM AND THE PHANTOM GOLD

BERKLEY BOOKS, NEW YORK

SLOCUM AND THE PHANTOM GOLD

A Berkley Book / published by arrangement with
the author

PRINTING HISTORY
Berkley edition / February 1994

ISBN: 0-425-14100-4

BERKLEY®
Berkley Books are published by The Berkley Publishing Group,
200 Madison Avenue, New York, New York 10016.
BERKLEY and the "B" design
are trademarks belonging to Berkley Publishing Corporation.

PRINTED IN THE UNITED STATES OF AMERICA

10 9 8 7 6 5 4 3 2 1

SLOCUM AND THE PHANTOM GOLD

1

John Slocum sneezed as flower pollen blew across the draw and into his face. Spring in western Idaho carried with it too many growing plants for his comfort. The harsh winter had faded, and runoff from the high peaks of the Bitterroot Mountains sent down floods of water that made flowers and trees bloom in wild profusion. Slocum sneezed again and wiped his nose on his bandanna, but his attention was focused on the purple-hazed distance.

"Perfect," he muttered. He patted his nervous Appaloosa's neck as he studied the road running from Coeur d'Alene toward Lewiston. It was hardly more than a double rut, turned to mud in many places. That made it attractive for Slocum's purposes. A stagecoach rattling along the road would have to slow down going through the mucky stretches or risk breaking an axle or getting the team bogged down.

When the coach slowed, Slocum would be ready with his six-shooter. There wasn't a single stagecoach running this route that wasn't creaking under the weight of too much gold. The Bitterroots were riddled with shafts dug by eager hard-rock miners. Some mines were independents, but most were owned by huge mining corporations that would never miss a few thousand dollars in gold dust.

A few pounds of gold would ride real pretty in Slocum's saddlebags and make him think life was worth living.

He sneezed again and settled down in the saddle. The spirited Appaloosa sidestepped a little. Slocum kept the big horse under control as he pictured the way the robbery would go. The stage couldn't gain any speed on the mud flat where he intended to rob it. The driver and guard would be more interested in finding a safe, dry route than in watching for road agents. Slocum saw the spot and knew he would be rich before the sun set.

That suited Slocum just fine. He had spent a hard winter in the mountains, laid up with a broken leg. He rubbed his right leg and shook his head, wondering how he had ever been so stupid as to agree to team up with Pierre Lacroix. The mad Frenchman had insisted there were beaver and bear and just about any other fur-bearing animal Slocum had ever heard of waiting to be skinned.

The market for fur wasn't what it had been, even five years back, but Slocum believed a good winter's work might earn him five hundred or even a thousand dollars. Reality had been different. The few fur-bearing animals they'd found had been scrawny, with pelts that hardly did their owners any good. Trying to sell them would have gotten Slocum laughed out of any reputable fur broker's auction. But he would have accepted a lost winter and even forgiven Lacroix if it hadn't been for the fall he had taken.

A snowbank had collapsed under him, and he slid more than forty feet down a mountainside. Lacroix had pulled him up and set his leg—and then abandoned him. Slocum had survived six weeks of winter, smoldering with hatred and vowing to get even with Lacroix. By spring thaw, Slocum was up and about.

He'd found he didn't have to even the score with his would-be partner. Slocum found Lacroix's body less than ten miles from their cabin. Whether the Frenchman had tried to go for help or had just upped and left, Slocum would never know. Pierre was dead, and the winter had been a complete failure.

He deserved this stagecoach robbery and the gold carried in the strongbox bolted to the inside floor.

"There it is," he said to the Appaloosa. The horse settled, sensing the importance of the next few minutes. "We're on our way to getting filthy rich." Slocum guided the horse down a winding, muddy path to the base of the hill where he had laid out the robbery. He wasn't in a hurry. There wasn't any need. The stagecoach would take more than an hour to reach the spot where he'd lighten their load.

Slocum took a wandering course to a tumble of boulders along the road. He figured this would provide cover until the stagecoach reached the mud flats where they would start to bog down.

His Appaloosa picked its way through the muck, then stopped abruptly, turning its head, ears pricked and listening hard. Slocum paused and pushed his Stetson back. He had learned the horse had good instincts. Something had caught the animal's attention.

On the brisk wind came faint sounds of harnesses rattling and horses neighing. Slocum smiled. The stagecoach was right on schedule. Then he heard something more that turned his stomach into a cold knot.

Gunfire. One shot. Another and another and a fourth. Then came the roar of a shotgun. From the thunderous report, it sounded as if a double-barreled shotgun had been fired—both barrels discharged at the same time.

Slocum checked the .37 caliber Colt Navy riding at his left hip in its cross-draw holster, then made sure his Winchester's magazine was filled. Only then did he put his heels to the horse's speckled flanks. More shots spurred his ride. He rounded the boulders he had planned to use as a hiding place and looked around.

A quarter mile back down the road he saw three men on horseback circling the stagecoach. The driver stood in his box with his hands up in the air. The guard lay sprawled over the edge of the box. From the crazy, boneless angle of the sprawl, the guard must be dead. And from inside the stagecoach came a piteous whine, like a whipped dog.

Slocum evaluated what was going on. He might drop back and follow the robbers. They would get careless if they didn't think a posse was hot on their trail. When they stopped to rest, they'd be easy prey. Slocum could get the gold from the coach without having to commit the actual robbery.

He changed his mind when he saw one highwayman empty his pistol into the passengers. Two men flopped out, dead. Another robber rode up and covered those still alive inside while the first robber reloaded. These weren't men intent on getting the gold and simply riding off to enjoy their ill-gotten gains. They were killers who took sick pleasure in murder. Slocum had seen their ilk during the war and they disgusted him.

He made sure his six-shooter rode easy, then he put his heels to his Appaloosa's flanks and sent the powerful horse racing toward the stagecoach. The robbers didn't see him until he was within a hundred yards. One turned and got off a quick shot in his direction. Slocum kept low over his horse's neck and kept riding. A hit from a pistol at this range depended more on luck than skill. Slocum rode hard until he got closer—much closer.

"Get him, Clem. Dammit, don't let him get us! He must be the law!" The robber trying to reload his pistol fumbled at the lead going into each chamber, dropping some of the bullets into the mud.

"Cain't. He's movin' too fast!" Clem's partner let off another round in Slocum's direction and then came up empty. The third robber was behind the stagecoach, and Slocum couldn't see him, but it was time for him to get his own six-shooter into action.

Less than ten yards away, Slocum whipped out his Colt Navy and got off two quick shots. Neither did more than scare the road agents' horses, but that was good enough. It gave the driver the chance to dive into the box and drag out his own rifle. He fired at the road agent hiding behind the stage.

"You miserable varmint!" the driver shouted. "You done up and kilt poor Tony. I'll see you in hell for that!" The driver fired several more times, none of his rounds doing more than spooking the robbers' horses.

Slocum got off one good shot that found a target in one of the road agent's legs. Clem yelped and bent over.

"Let's get outta here. That's gotta be the law! There's a whole damn posse with him!" The third robber rounded the back of the stage and got off a wild shot. Slocum turned his Colt Navy in the man's direction, but his round dug a splinter out of the stagecoach's frame rather than burying itself in flesh.

The three robbers hightailed it through the mud, kicking up a spray of muck that obscured their retreat. Slocum emptied his Colt, then drew his Winchester and started slow firing after the road agents. His Appaloosa was starting to crowhop from all the shooting, which made Slocum's chances of hitting any of the fleeing men difficult.

"Take that, you mangy cayuses!" shouted the driver. The hammer of his rifle slammed down on an empty chamber.

The man didn't seem to notice. He kept cocking his rifle and dry-firing it until the robbers had vanished into the foothills.

As suddenly as the carnage had started, it was over. Slocum sat on his horse and stared into the distance. The Bitterroot Mountains were as lovely as ever, draped in winter snows and purple distance. The wind still carried the pollen that made him sneeze, but now gunpowder and the acrid copper tang of spilled blood were added to the mix.

"Want me to go after them?" he called to the driver. Slocum wasn't sure if the robbers had gotten anything from the stage. If they had, he could take the gold from the bloody-handed robbers and keep on riding.

If not, Slocum considered robbing the stage and hightailing it himself.

"No need, mister. You come along just in time. Those murderin' swine would have killed us all!"

Slocum turned when the stage's door creaked open. A woman stepped out into the mud. For a moment, all thought of robbery left his mind. He might have seen a lovelier woman sometime, but he couldn't remember exactly when. He'd thought Lotta Crabtree had been pretty when he saw her over in Virginia City, but that talented young performer couldn't hold a candle to the woman on this stage.

"Thank you, sir," the woman said. Slocum heard silver bells along with the gentle whistle of wind past the stagecoach when she spoke. She looked up at him with eyes bluer than the wide sky. Strands of hair so blond it was almost white in the sun fluttered out from under a white traveling bonnet. High cheek-bones gave the woman a regal look. She was high-class and definitely out of place in the middle of the Idaho wilderness.

"Ma'am," Slocum said, tipping his hat. "Pleased to be of service."

"They shot the men in the coach with me," she said in a steady voice. From the paleness and way she wobbled, Slocum saw the murders had shaken the young woman's confidence, but he liked the way she refused to give in to fragility, as many of her hothouse sisters might have.

"I'll see to them," Slocum said, dismounting. As he hitched his horse's reins to the rear wheel of the stage, he knew he wasn't going to steal the gold. He had somehow become the savior instead of the robber.

He pulled open the door and saw two men sprawled gracelessly inside. The road agents had made quick work of both men. One had two holes in his head. For all the gore spattered against the stagecoach's interior, the victims weren't actually bleeding much. Slocum grabbed one man's collar and pulled him out onto the ground. The other man was bloodier, having been shot through the chest. Slocum got him out, too.

The driver had already pulled the first man around to the rear of the stage and was struggling to get the body into the boot, next to the luggage. Slocum added the second man. They wouldn't care if they rode second class now.

"It is your bravery that saved our lives. Thank you again," the woman said. Slocum turned. The young woman was taller than he had thought. Her blue eyes were only a few inches lower than his own, and he topped six feet. She smiled almost shyly and thrust out her hand impetuously. "My name is Lurene Macmillan, and I am on my way to Precious."

"Precious?" Slocum asked. Then he remembered. It was a small mining town stuffed up in the foothills of the Bitterroots. It didn't amount to a hill of beans, from all he had heard. Why such a beautiful woman was going there was beyond him.

"Would you be so kind as to accompany us, sir?" the blond asked. "I would consider it a great favor." She batted her long eyelashes a little, and Slocum knew he wasn't thinking straight when he agreed.

His green eyes darted to the iron box bolted to the floor of the stagecoach's compartment. The road agents hadn't had time to blow it open and take the gold inside. How much was being transported?

"They didn't get a plugged nickel, thanks to you, mister," said the driver. Slocum looked up to the driver's box and saw the grizzled driver pushing cartridges into his rifle. He wouldn't be dry-firing now if Slocum took it into his head to finish the job the others had started. The way the driver kept the rifle aimed in Slocum's general direction said he didn't trust his savior too much.

"Please, do accompany us into Precious," Lurene Macmillan begged. "I'd consider it a *personal* favor."

Slocum wasn't much sure what his reward would be, but the robbery was long past. He would have to find some other way of making a few dollars now.

A slow smile crossed his face. There would be other stagecoaches with more gold. These mountains were covered with mines. Being broke for day or two more wouldn't matter much to him.

"I'd consider it an honor to escort you into town. I was heading that way myself." Slocum saw the skeptical expression on the driver's face. Slocum didn't even know exactly in what direction Precious lay, but he guessed it would take some backtracking on his part to get there.

"Why don't you go on ahead and do some scouting?" suggested the driver. He didn't want Slocum and his quick six-shooter behind him.

Slocum tipped his hat in Lurene Macmillan's direction again, mounted, and started down the trail trying to figure out from the tracks in the mud where the road to Precious might lay. He found a signpost that had fallen down. From the look of the terrain, he figured that Precious was off to the north. He waited for the stagecoach to catch up. The driver whipped the horses and got through the mud flats and started up a poorly traveled track, confirming Slocum's guess.

For the rest of the afternoon, he rode back and forth, scouting ahead and then dropping back to ride alongside the coach, catching Lurene's smile and flashing eyes. Slocum conjured up all sorts of fantasies. He had spent a winter with a trapper and the last two months snowed in and alone with a broken leg. Any woman would look like a fairy-tale princess to him. It just happened he had come across a woman who really was comely.

The peaks began rising like stony daggers on either side of the road and somewhere around four o'clock the sun dipped behind the mountains and cast twilight shadows everywhere. The small town of Precious was nestled in the foothills. The surrounding peaks were dotted with dozens of shafts that vanished into the rock. Precious might be well named if even half of those mines produced high-grade ore.

"Yee-haw!" shouted the driver as he whipped his team into the town. The sudden burst of speed took Slocum by surprise. He followed the stagecoach more slowly and saw the driver had reined back in front of the stage office.

By the time Slocum dismounted and went over to the stage, the bodies of the two passengers had been pulled out of the boot and the guard had been lowered to a bench in front of the office. Slocum wanted to talk more with Lurene Macmillian and find out why she had come to this jerkwater town. He looked around and decided it wasn't even that. There wasn't a train serving Precious.

When Slocum heard a six-shooter cock behind him, he froze. His hand twitched slightly. He wondered if he could draw and turn and fire before a slug ripped apart his spine.

"Keep movin', mister," came the cold tone behind him. Slocum waited for the six-shooter's muzzle to press into his back, but the man behind him was too cagy. A strong hand grabbed his shoulder and guided him forward. The leveled pistol was in the other hand, just beyond any hope of knocking it off target.

"Marshal," called the agent from the stage office, "they done upped and killed *three* men. Two of 'em were *passengers*. How long you goin' to let this thievin' go on?"

"Mr. Lucas, you know there's not much I can do about it," the marshal said. Slocum shifted slightly and was rewarded with a tighter grip on his shoulder, holding him in place. He had worried that the town's lawman might be the one with the gun pointed at him. His worst fear had been realized.

Slocum hadn't gone through the West without causing a ruckus. Wanted posters for a dozen crimes carried his name and likeness. He had committed some of the crimes; others he hadn't. To a small-town marshal, it might not much matter. The rewards would look mighty good to a man who didn't make fifty dollars a month in paper money.

And there was one charge that Slocum would never be able to escape. During the war he had ridden with Quantrill's Raiders. When the 150 men in Lawrence, Kansas, had been slaughtered, he hadn't protested too much. Slocum was no namby-pamby. He had done his share of killing, but Quantrill and Bloody Bill Anderson had gone too far when they slaughtered innocent women and children, too.

They had gut-shot Slocum and left him for dead. By the time he had recovered and returned to his family farm in Calhoun, Georgia, his parents were dead and a carpetbagger judge was looking with greedy eyes on the land. Slocum had cut down the judge and his hired gun when they'd ridden out to seize the land. And he had been dogged by the charge of judge killing ever since.

It didn't matter if the carpetbagger judge had deserved what he got. Slocum was guilty of the crime, and eager bounty hunters had been on his trail ever since.

Was Precious's town marshal the kind of lawman who spent much time riffling through old wanted posters? Slocum's fingers twitched as he thought again about going for his six-shooter.

"If you don't do something soon about those thieves, Marshal, you ain't gonna be reelected," opined one of the crowd gathered to see what the commotion was about. Others agreed. This made Slocum even edgier. A town marshal who might lose his job tended to be even more trigger-happy than usual.

"Why ever are you holding a gun on this man, Marshal?" demanded Lurene Macmillan. She stood with her hands balled into tight fists, which were balanced on generously flaring hips. "If it wasn't for him, we would all be dead."

"That's right, Marshal. He done saved us out there," spoke up the driver.

"Maybe we ought to hire *him* as marshal," the stage agent said.

"That's all right. No harm done," Slocum said, easing away from the marshal and the gun pointed at his back. With some reluctance, the marshal holstered his six-shooter, but the way he studied Slocum hinted at recognition nibbling at the edges of the lawman's mind.

Slocum turned, intending to get away as quickly as he could, but then stopped and looked around as resolve hardened to finish what he had started. He had wanted to talk with Lurene Macmillan once more before getting the hell out of Precious. But the woman had vanished into thin air.

2

"If you don't stop them road agents, it'll be on your head," the driver said to the town marshal. Slocum saw this didn't set well with the lawman, who nervously rubbed his strong, thick fingers along the butt of his well-used six-gun.

Even worse, the marshal's eyes kept coming back to light on Slocum's face. The lawman was trying hard to remember where he had seen Slocum before. It wouldn't take much for him to go back to his clapboard office across the street and start leafing through wanted posters. He was bound to find something interesting. Then it would be time for Slocum to either shoot his way out of town or go to the gallows.

He started sidling away when the crowd pushed between him and the marshal. He wanted to talk to Lurene Macmillan one more time. There was something captivating about the woman's smile, the glint in her pure blue eyes, the way she spoke and carried herself. And Slocum had to admit to more than a passing curiosity about what brought the woman to a godforsaken place like Precious, Idaho.

"Stop! You, there! Stop!"

Slocum froze, his hand on the ebony butt of his Colt Navy. The shooting might start sooner than he'd anticipated. He saw the stagecoach agent and the driver standing side by side. The driver was pointing squarely at him.

"You, mister, come on over here," the agent urged. There wasn't any hint of malice in Lucas's words. Slocum took the chance that it was better talking to the agent than to the marshal, who was engaged with several people. From the snippets he overheard, one of the dead passengers had a wife and she was berating the marshal something fierce for allowing murder on the roads near Precious.

"This is the young fella," the driver said gruffly. "When I first set eyes on him, I thought he was another of them road agents."

Slocum said nothing. He wondered if the driver knew how close he came to the truth.

"The Precious and Coeur d'Alene Stagecoach Lines would like to present this reward as a token of our thanks," Lucas said, fumbling in his vest pocket. He rummaged around, pushed aside a big railroad watch, and then pulled out a rumpled greenback. "I know it's not much, but we're not a rich company."

Slocum accepted the crumpled five dollar bill from the agent. He stared at it in wonder. If he had his druthers, he'd take what was inside the strongbox, but that wasn't possible now. Slocum had intended to get rich today and had ended up with five dollars in virtually worthless paper money.

"Thanks," Slocum said. He started to turn down the money, then decided five dollars were better than the holes he had in his pocket. This wouldn't make him rich, but it would buy him a meal and a drink and maybe let him into a poker game at one of the dozen saloons lining the town's main street.

"If you're lookin' for work," the driver said, clearing his throat loudly and making sure the marshal overheard, "we got a guard's job open."

"The pay isn't much," the agent rattled on, ignoring the driver. "We can only offer ten dollars a trip between here and Coeur d'Alene. And you have to supply your own weapons." Lucas looked at the worn ebony butt on Slocum's Colt Navy. The agent smiled a little. "I reckon that wouldn't be much of a problem."

"Thanks for the offer," Slocum said. "I might just take you up on it, if I can't find other work around town." He was aware of the marshal glaring at him as he turned and went in search of Lurene Macmillan. Staying around this town long wasn't in the cards, but Slocum thought he was safe enough for the evening.

In spite of the spring flowers blooming all around, it was still closer to winter than summer. A cold wind whipped off the snow high up in the Bitterroot Mountains and made Slocum pull his duster closer for warmth. He kept an eye out for the young blond but didn't see her. There were only a few boardinghouses in town, and all had No Vacancy signs posted prominently. The two hotels Slocum saw just off the main street didn't look to be the kind of place a genteel woman would stay.

One advertised sleeping space for fifty cents a night. Glancing through the open front door, Slocum saw the men stacked like cordwood inside. If one turned over, the man at the far side of the room would know it. Slocum reckoned all three floors of rooms in the brick hotel were like this. Most boomtowns had trouble keeping up with the flood of men coming to find their fortunes in the ground. Precious was no different.

The other hotel was more traditional, having individual rooms, but Slocum saw that they were occupied by whores. The painted women came and went constantly, looking like a line of ants as they entered nearby dancehalls and returned quickly with their current paramour.

A lady, a real lady, wasn't likely to stay at a hotel filled with cribs. Somehow, Slocum had Lurene Macmillan pegged as having more culture than anyone else in Precious.

So why was she here?

Slocum found a small café and ate a quiet meal. It took two of his dollars, but he felt worlds better having a hot meal of elk stew with carrots and potatoes swimming alongside the meat and hot biscuits with peach jam. The coffee that washed it down left a bitter taste; he guessed it wasn't as much coffee as it was boiled root. That didn't matter. He had spent the six weeks when he was laid up eating little more than maggot-filled pork and hardtack.

He went out into the main street, stretched, and looked around. The choice of saloons showed that this was a mining town. Men working underground for sixteen backbreaking hours a day needed harsh whiskey to dull the pain of living.

Slocum strolled over to the Gold Tooth Saloon, it being the nearest. A wave of smoke and heat billowed out into his face. He peered through the swinging doors and saw several card games in progress. A bored woman called keno at the back, and two professional gamblers with their black coats and slicked-back hair dealt faro. Slocum wasn't interested in any of those games. He preferred to feel the slide of the cards himself and follow the betting of stud poker.

"Welcome to the Gold Tooth, mister. Have a drink," greeted the barkeep. The portly man with the heavily waxed mustache waved Slocum over to the bar. He had a drink waiting by the time Slocum bellied up. "Heard all about how you saved the stage. I'm much obliged."

"How's that?" Slocum asked, gingerly sampling the liquor. To his surprise, it went down smooth as silk. He had thought he'd be served some rotgut laced with nitric acid.

"Yeast," the barkeep said. When he saw Slocum frown, he explained. "I had a box of yeast shipped over from Coeur d'Alene. I'm makin' my own beer, and I need it for the brewin'. Hell, the whole town thanks you. When I finish, I'll have the best damned beer in all of Idaho!"

Slocum scratched his head in wonder. He had wanted gold from the shipment and the saloon owner had wanted a box filled with yeast to make beer. Looking around, Slocum wasn't so sure that the barkeep didn't have the right idea. The yeast was worth more than its weight in gold. A thousand dollars a month might change hands buying fresh-brewed beer.

"Don't think anything about it. I was just passing by," Slocum said.

"Anything you want, just let me know," the barkeep said.

"One thing," Slocum said as the man started away. "What can you tell me about the passengers? I didn't have much chance to talk to them."

"Reckon not, since two of them was dead as mackerels," the barkeep laughed. "One was a local store owner. Gimpy O'Leary ran a bookstore. The only one, truth to tell. He was on a buying trip, or so he told his old lady."

"She the one giving the marshal hell for letting him get killed on the stage?" asked Slocum.

"None other. Mrs. O'Leary is a feisty one. Don't know any man in Precious who'd want to try taming her, though there's a real drought of womenfolk hereabouts."

"What of the others?" Slocum urged, hoping the barkeep knew something about Lurene Macmillan.

"Another was a drummer, I heard tell. He was the one what got drilled in the head. Seems the stage company's claiming all his traveling stock is theirs, and Lucas is trying to sell it to one of our two general stores."

"Lucas the stage agent?"

"None other. I swear, that man is so tight he can squeeze a nickel and make the buffalo squeal. Surprised the hell out of me, niggardly old Lucas giving you a five dollar reward and all."

Slocum saw that nothing went past the saloon owner. He kept his peace and waited. The man had to know he wanted to find out more about the only other passenger, who was not only the prettiest one but the only one to survive.

"Then there was Miss Macmillan," the barkeep said, his eyes narrowing a mite. "Heard she was coming here to find her brother. Had some news from Saint Louis, Lucas said. Don't rightly know what that would be."

"So her brother's in Precious?" Slocum said, hoping to prime the pump. Nothing seemed forthcoming until he indicated he wanted a shot of whiskey. This time he paid for it with one of the bills he had received in change at the café. It didn't much surprise him to find that the liquor cost him four bits. The price of whiskey—and information—came high on the frontier.

"Suppose that's right." the barkeep said. "Haven't heard of any miner named Macmillan, but then there's so danged many of them, who's to know?"

Slocum had to be content with this scrap of information. He sipped at the whiskey and looked around, watching the play at the tables.

"You a gamblin' man?" the barkeep asked after he had made his rounds up and down the long bar.

"Been known to make a bet or two in the right game," Slocum allowed. The barkeep grinned broadly, and Slocum saw where the name of the saloon came from. A huge gold tooth shone in the owner's mouth.

"I can use another dealer. Those two are cheating me something fierce." The barkeep pointed at the two gamblers working the faro games. "Don't know how, exactly, but they are."

Slocum shrugged noncommittally. If the saloon owner wasn't able to tell how the men were cheating, it wasn't his place to let him know. From casual observation, Slocum saw the pair was doing more to cheat the customers than the house. Chips would get paid out fairly enough, but somehow one or two would slip back into the gambler's own pile. It didn't take that much effort to palm a chip when most of the miners at the table were more interested in getting drunk and bragging about their claims than gambling.

"I'll see how it goes and let you know," Slocum said. He was proving to be a popular fellow. He hadn't been in Precious for more than two hours, and he had received two job offers. Slocum wasn't likely to take either of them, but too often he had gone for months searching for work and hadn't found it.

He watched the cards slip and slid across one green felt covered table until he had some idea about the other players. All were drunker than lords and nobody paid much attention to odds. This was the kind of game that Slocum could make a quick twenty dollars in.

"You gents mind if I sit in?" He pointed to an empty chair.

"Come on in," greeted one. The skeletally thin man across the table stiffened.

"No!" the corpselike man said. "We got enough in the game now."

"I'm just being friendly, Carson. You can be such a mean skunk. Show some neighborly affection for your fellow man," urged the first. He hiccupped and took a long drink from the bottle at his elbow, then offered Slocum a pull.

Slocum settled down, accepted the drink, taking only a small amount of the fiery liquor, and said, "Much obliged.

Precious surely is a friendly place."

The cadaverous man across the table only glared. Slocum settled down to playing the penny ante game of draw poker, winning a pot or two and losing even more just to keep the others happy. Small losses now and then meant nothing if he won the few bigger pots. And he did.

The miners with him were a sociable lot, except for Carson. They laughed, joked, and didn't much care that their piles of chips slowly vanished as they played.

Slocum wiped sweat off his face, then shucked of his heavy canvas duster. He hung it on the chair behind him and got back to playing. He had a decent hand and thought he could win a pot of almost six dollars.

But it didn't work out that way. Carson won, and shot him a cold stare. For the first time, Slocum began studying the gaunt miner. Carson was nowhere near as drunk as he was pretending. His thin fingers stroked the edges of the cards with sure, deliberate movement. Sitting stolidly, he was taking in everything and only pretending to drink every time the bottle made its way around the table. Like Slocum, he was in the game to win serious money. And that put the two men directly at odds with each other.

Slocum wondered if Carson's continual fingering of the cards meant the deck had been shaved. He slid his own fingers over them, looking for telltale cuts or marks. He found nothing. But if Carson had shaved the deck, that meant he could deal whatever card he wanted. Slocum began watching more carefully—but his attention drifted away when he had the feeling of being watched.

Looking up, he saw the town marshal standing just inside the door. The lawman's hot eyes bored into him. Slocum tried not to show that he noticed the scrutiny, but he did. Had the marshal gone through his wanted posters? Slocum damned himself for wanting to stick around Precious and talk with Lurene Macmillan one more time. He was pushing his luck, and he knew it now.

Slocum lost two small pots through uneasiness over the vulturelike stare, then noticed that the marshal had vanished. If the man had found anything indicting Slocum, he would have arrested him right away. Slocum settled down again and won a large pot, almost ten dollars.

For his effort, Slocum got a nasty look from Carson.

"You seem to be winnin' more 'n your fair share," Carson said in a gravelly voice. Slocum watched the miner's Adam's apple bob up and down like a cork in a stream swelled by spring runoff.

"No more than you," Slocum observed. The number of chips in front of each of them was about the same.

"I'm a local. You ain't."

"What's the difference? He's a good fellow well met, hale and stout," laughed the man to Slocum's right. Then he fell out of his chair and lay on the floor, snoring loudly.

The other three men in the game took scant notice. They were beginning to bet wildly, the liquor fogging their good sense. Slocum and Carson began fighting over the pots, playing their cards carefully. Slocum won more than he lost, and he began taking some of the chips from Carson's stash.

It was then that Slocum saw Carson use the shaved deck to his advantage, dealing himself three aces. Slocum folded and sat back, his cold green eyes boring into Carson. The miner began squirming under the glacial stare. Carson turned even paler when Slocum pushed back from the table and touched the butt of his Colt Navy. Carson folded suddenly and grabbed his chips.

He almost ran from the saloon.

"Looks like the game is over, gents," Slocum said. He counted his chips and saw he had won almost forty dollars. Feeling expansive, he said, "Let me buy you all a drink."

The others eagerly accepted his offer and downed the whiskey Slocum bought. He finished off another drink and turned to leave the Gold Tooth, then remembered his duster.

"Who took my duster?" he demanded. He had hung it on the back of his chair at the card table. It was gone.

Before anyone could answer, a gunshot rang out. Another followed. It took Slocum a second to realize the reports came from outside the saloon. He joined the rush outside.

"What happened? Where's the fight?" someone called. The answers were jumbled and slurred from too much booze. Then the crowd surged and moved into the street. Someone let out a cry and several men broke off from the throng.

Three men hurried into an alley and crouched over a man lying face down in the mud. One man rolled the corpse over, wiped off the muck, studied the face, and then looked up to tell everyone, "It's Kenny Moore. He's stone dead!"

Slocum caught his breath. The dead man wore his duster and had been shot twice in the middle of the back.

3

Slocum looked around, even though he knew the back shooter wasn't likely to stay around. He didn't see anyone who might have gunned down the man who had stolen his duster. Slocum moved aside when the marshal shoved through the crowd.

"What's going on here?" the lawman demanded.

"Marshal Kent, somebody done upped and dry-gulched him." The man who had wiped the mud off the murdered man's face rolled the body over with his toe. "What are you going to do about it?"

"Let me see." The marshal knelt and tried to make sense out of the muddy corpse. He found the bullet holes in the man's back. Kent's eyes flashed around the circle of men staring down at him, but his gaze settled on John Slocum.

"You," Marshal Kent said. "Let me see your hogleg."

"What's that going to prove?" Slocum asked. "You know I used the gun this afternoon."

"Maybe you didn't take time to reload after you gunned down Moore here." The marshal stood and widened his stance, pulling his jacket away from his holstered six-shooter.

"I was inside the Gold Tooth when he was killed. Ask

anybody. I was buying drinks for some of them." Slocum waited for the corroboration. It was slow in coming, but when it did, he was glad to see it was the saloon's owner who stood up for him.

"You're barkin' up the wrong tree, Marshal," said the barkeep. "I was servin' him when the first shot went off. And danged near everyone else can testify that he was still at the bar when the second shot was fired."

"That's so. I saw him, too." "He's okay, Marshal." "Who really kilt Kenny?" came the murmurs from the crowd.

Slocum relaxed when Kent backed off.

"You need to find who's killing up on the streets, Marshal," said the barkeep. "If you can't do it, maybe we ought to oust you and find someone who can." The saloon owner turned and smiled broadly. His gold tooth flashed in the dim light coming from inside the saloon. Slocum sucked in his breath. He didn't want anyone nominating him to take over the law-keeping job in Precious.

"The marshal's the right man for this job," Slocum said suddenly. Kent's eyes widened in surprise, then narrowed as he looked at Slocum as if he were a bug that had just crawled into his coffee cup. "He knows the folks hereabout and who's most likely to do something like this. I'm just passing through."

"We need to get up a vigilance committee," suggested the saloon owner. "We can patrol our own streets and keep them from gunning us down like that." The barkeep pointed toward the body in the alley next to his saloon.

A general rumble of agreement passed through the crowd. Marshal Kent stirred them up and pushed them back. Slocum wondered if he ought to reclaim his duster, then saw the two ragged holes in the back and the blood that had soaked into the canvas. He wasn't too keen on putting the duster back on. Slocum let the crowd carry him along into the heat of the Gold Tooth Saloon.

He didn't take part as the natural leaders came forth and presented their notions about patrolling the streets to keep them safe for law-abiding citizens. The vigilance committee formed slowly, but along lines Slocum had seen dozens of times. He didn't cotton much to people taking the law into their own hands like this. Vigilantes easily turned into lynch mobs. And vigilantes didn't much care who they strung up.

"Is there a judge in Precious?" he asked the barkeep.

"Nope, none. We're not even on a judicial circuit. If we want justice served here, we got to go over to Coeur d'Alene. Some folks think we're lucky just to have a town marshal."

"And you? What do you think?"

"I think that was your duster Moore was wearing. I didn't see him swipe it, but I do remember it hangin' on the back of your chair." The saloon owner eyed Slocum significantly, then went off to serve more whiskey.

Slocum heaved a deep breath and thought on it. Moore might have been a sneak thief and have racked up dozens of enemies over his petty crimes. It might have been payback time for some other iniquity. But another suspicion kept pushing this comfortable notion out of Slocum's head. Whoever had cut down Kenny Moore might have mistaken him for John Slocum.

It was time to leave Precious and keep on riding. Slocum had enough of a poke now to keep him happy and in grub for a while. He might even be able to get honest work over in Lewiston or Coeur d'Alene. His leg had healed enough for him to do almost anything.

"Thanks for the drink," Slocum said, putting the shot glass back on the bar. The barkeep smiled and waved to him, then went back to arguing over the organization of the vigilance committee. To Slocum's way of thinking, organizing a bunch of vigilantes was the same as trying to establish pecking order among a flock of vultures.

He stopped in the door and felt the cold wind blowing in his face. The Gold Tooth Saloon was hot inside and the sudden change in temperature made him shiver. Slocum stepped out of the door, suddenly aware that he was silhouetted. If the unknown gunman had wanted to kill him, he would have presented a better target than Kenny Moore's back.

"What's going on inside?" came the level tones of Marshal Kent. "They got their lynch mob formed yet?"

"You don't care much for vigilance committees, do you?" responded Slocum. He saw the marshal sitting in a chair to the right of the swinging doors, tipped back on the chair's rickety rear legs. The lawman was smoking a cheroot. He silently offered Slocum one.

Slocum wanted out of town, but he knew better than to push matters too much with the lawman. He accepted the smoke, settled down in the chair next to him, and lit the cheroot. The smoke flowed into his lungs and brought him fully awake. Slocum hadn't realized how groggy he was getting inside the hot saloon.

"Too much rotgut will put you to sleep," the marshal said, as if reading Slocum's mind.

"It's been a spell since I unrolled my blanket," Slocum admitted.

The marshal puffed on his smoke for a spell, then said, "I been going through my wanted posters. I've got a good memory for faces and thought I remembered yours."

"So?" Slocum didn't make any sudden moves. If the marshal had wanted to arrest him, he would have come on with his six-shooter drawn.

"So I don't much think killing a carpetbagger judge is a

crime. I'm from Georgia, myself. You got any other warrants chasin' after you?"

"I'd be a damned fool to tell you, if I had," Slocum said.

"Reckon so." Kent puffed a bit more, tapped the ash from the end of the cheroot, and then said, "I don't much care what's gone on before you got to Precious. I'm more interested in stopping what most folks see as out-of-control crime."

"I just got here. Can't help you on that score." Slocum was getting antsy to leave Precious.

"You have the look of a man accustomed to using that six-shooter of yours. I'm offering you a job as deputy. Don't pay much, but you'd be doing some good." The marshal looked at him, but Slocum couldn't read the man's expression. Slocum didn't think Kent was blackmailing him into taking the job, though mention of the wanted poster hinted at it.

"All I intend to do is leave town, Marshal," said Slocum.

"That was your duster Kenny was wearing. I remember seeing you with it when you rode into town. How'd he end up wearing your clothing?"

"He stole it," Slocum said.

Kent made a snorting noise. "Figures. Kenny had sticky fingers. Maybe it finally caught up with him."

"Maybe," Slocum said, knowing the marshal didn't believe that for an instant.

"See you around, Slocum," said the lawman. He kicked to standing and walked off, never looking back.

Slocum finished his smoke, wondering what was going on in Precious. To hear the townspeople talk, crime was so widespread they had to take matters into their own hands. As far as he could tell, Precious wasn't much different from any other boomtown.

Getting up, Slocum started off to find where he had left his Appaloosa tethered near the stage depot. As he walked, he heard rapid footsteps behind him. Slocum kept walking until he came even with a dark alleyway. He ducked in, spun, and grabbed at his pursuer.

A loud shriek cut through the night air, and Slocum found himself with an armful of struggling woman.

"Lurene!" he exclaimed. Slocum released her and stepped back.

She started to say something, but no words came out. She straightened her skirts and patted her blond hair back into place before getting settled enough to speak.

"Mr. Slocum, how glad I am that it was you who grabbed me."

"I'm sorry. I heard someone behind me." He didn't go on to tell her he worried about the back shooter discovering his mistake earlier with Kenny Moore and coming after the duster's real owner.

"It was all my fault. I should never have—I—oh, it's so terrible!" Lurene Macmillan sank down to her knees amid voluminous skirts and buried her face in her cupped hands. Her entire body shook with the intensity of her crying.

"What's wrong?" Slocum asked. "I apologized for frightening you."

"That's not it, Mr. Slocum."

"Please, call me John."

"John," she said, looking up with tear-filled blue eyes. "He's dead!"

"I know," Slocum said, the image of the man facedown in the mud returning to haunt him.

"You do? How? I only saw him four hours ago at his claim, and it took me so long to get back to town. I got lost in the dark and took the wrong road and—"

"Who are you talking about?" Slocum asked, cutting her off. Lurene was babbling, and he was confused. It sounded as if Lurene meant someone else had died tonight. If there had been two deaths in Precious, the vigilance committee might be right about nipping the crimes in the bud. Most frontier towns didn't see a killing a month, much less two in one night.

"My brother is dead. Murdered! They shot him down like he was some sort of mad dog! He was the kindest man alive and they slaughtered him!"

"Who killed your brother?" Slocum took a deep breath, then helped Lurene stand. "Tell me everything."

"Very well," she said, sniffing hard. Lurene dabbed at her eyes and wiped her nose with a lace handkerchief she had tucked in her sleeve. She took a deep breath to calm herself, and Slocum couldn't help noticing the way her breasts rose and fell so delightfully. He forced his attention to what the young woman was saying.

"I came to Precious to tell my brother of our parents' deaths. They died of cholera. It was terrible. It killed many people along the river in Saint Louis."

"I heard tell of the epidemic. Spread all the way down the Mississippi to New Orleans," he said. This had been last year. Lurene was slow getting the news to her brother, if it was the same cholera epidemic.

"I caught the disease, also. It took me some time to recuperate. I wanted to come tell Charles the details. A telegram seemed so—so cold. And I wanted to reassure him I was fully recovered."

"You got here and he was dead?"

"Claim jumpers murdered him!" she said hotly.

"How do you know?"

"Why, I know where his claim was. I went out—I rented a buckboard and team and rode out—and saw him. He greeted me. We talked of family matters and then, they, they—"

Lurene broke down again. Slocum held her in his arms, noting how nicely her curves fit his.

"Men rode up and just gunned him down?"

"Yes! I was in his cabin. Shack, really. It was drafty and perfectly awful. I don't know how Charles survived the winter there."

"The killers," Slocum urged. He didn't know where this was heading, but he could guess and knew he was a fool for not turning tail and running like a scalded hog.

"They rode in and murdered him. They didn't see me, I don't think. If they had, they would have murdered me, too." Lurene pushed back from Slocum and boldly met his gaze. She was becoming defiant now that the initial shock and fear were wearing off.

"You'd better tell the marshal about it. Kent seems like an honorable man," said Slocum.

"He won't do anything about this. It's out of his jurisdiction. I went straight to him, then I spent almost an hour here in town hunting for you."

"I can't do anything about this." Slocum remembered how Kent had offered him the job of deputy. He hadn't accepted the marshal's offer to enforce the law, and he wasn't going to take the law into his own hands to find the killer of Lurene's brother.

"But you're the only one I know here. You're the only one I can trust." Lurene sounded more aggrieved than frightened now. She couldn't believe he would turn her down.

"I'm not a hired gun. I don't kill people because someone pays me."

"Really, John, that's not what I want at all!" Lurene stamped her foot in anger. "I need your help in establishing Charles's claim. They killed him to take his mine. They are claim jumpers!"

"If you have your bother's registered deed, that's all you need."

"It—it's in the cabin and I forgot to take it. Charles showed it to me. He put it in a Clabber Girl Baking Soda can and hid it under the floorboard near his stove. If you can get it, that will prove those killers stole the LuLu Belle!"

"That's the name of his mine?"

"Yes, the LuLu Belle. I don't know how he decided on such a common name, and I never asked." Lurene sniffed. "I never had the chance. And now he's gone, just like our parents."

Slocum fought a brief battle with himself, and figured he lost when he heard himself saying, "Where's this LuLu Belle mine? I can go out and look it over and maybe find the deed."

"Oh, John, thank you!"

Lurene threw her arms around his neck and pulled him close for a quick kiss. She jumped back as if burned. Proper young ladies didn't do such things in public. Lurene looked around guiltily, but no one walked the streets at this time of night.

"Do you have a place to stay?" Slocum asked, remembering the dearth of hotels.

"I can stay at Mrs. Addington's Boardinghouse on the outskirts of town."

Slocum hadn't seen it but knew there must be some place were a genteel young woman might stay, even in a wide-open mining town like Precious.

"I'm not making any promises," he said, wondering just what he had gotten himself into.

"Don't risk your life, John. We can get a posse together or something and throw those killers out, if necessary. But I don't want them destroying the deed before then." Lurene paused a moment and added, "I can't ask you to do this for nothing. You're too generous a man to demand payment, but—"

"But what?" he said more brusquely than he'd intended. Slocum was angry at himself for sticking his nose into a mess that was none of his doing.

"I'll give you half the claim. Charles said the LuLu Belle wasn't wildly rich, but it provided him a decent living. That should make it worth your while."

"That's not necessary. I don't want half," Slocum said. "Keep it. You'll probably need all the money you can come by."

"I insist. Half," Lurene said firmly. Slocum shrugged. If she wanted to make him a mine owner for his trouble, he wasn't going to argue the point.

"I'll be waiting, John. Please be careful." Lurene looked around and saw no one. She gave him another kiss, this time more than the frightened peck lavished on him before. For this alone Slocum would have ridden through hell for the young woman.

He left Lurene Macmillan and walked slowly toward his horse. The Appaloosa stood patiently, tugging slightly at the reins to get to a watering trough. Slocum mounted and hesitated for a moment. He could ride deeper into the Bitterroot Mountains and find Charles Macmillan's claim and the men who had killed him, or he could retrace the route he had taken earlier and just ride on.

Slocum shook his head. Nothing today had worked out the way he'd intended. A simple robbery had turned into a rescue and a five dollar reward from the stagecoach company's agent. And someone wearing his duster had been shot down. Now he was riding to a distant mining claim to retrieve the deed hidden under the floorboards for a lovely blond he had only just met.

Some days were downright unpredictable.

Riding slowly, Slocum found the trail leading back into the mountains. He picked up the pace when the moon rose and gave a better view of the rocky road. He saw signs of the recent passage of a buckboard, giving credence to Lurene's story. Slocum tried not to doubt everything told him, but he had learned caution. Even the simplest of statements might be laden with lies.

Lurene Macmillan was telling the truth, at least about coming this way earlier.

Slocum fell into the rocking rhythm of riding, almost drifting off to sleep. It had been too many hours since he'd slept and fatigue was catching up with him. Facing down claim jumpers with bleary eyes wasn't a good idea, but Slocum didn't intend a frontal assault.

He'd find the LuLu Belle Mine, sneak in and fetch the claim for Lurene, and be on his way before any of the murderous claim jumpers even knew he was within ten miles. That was his plan. And it went south when he heard the scrape of leather boot soles against rock.

Slocum snapped upright in the saddle, eyes wide and heart pounding. The sound of someone moving on rock above him was unmistakable. He swung to face the hidden man.

He saw the muzzle flash before he heard the report or felt the bullet rip across his forehead. Slocum tumbled from the saddle and hit the rocky ground.

He didn't move.

4

Pain exploded like Fourth of July fireworks in Slocum's head. He moaned and rolled to his side. He thought the top of his head was going to fall off and spill his brains all over the road. Gingerly, he touched his forehead and felt the sticky trail of oozing blood. New waves of pain and a flow of blood into his eyes robbed him of vision when he tried to sit up.

Blind, confused, and in agony from the shallow groove across his forehead, Slocum tried to remember what had happened.

"Bushwhacker," he muttered. Even as the memory returned, so did his caution. Slocum threw himself back to the ground and rolled fast and hard until he fetched up against a large rock. The impact caused a new set of aches and pains to run through him, but whoever had tried to kill him must be watching.

Slocum worked to get the blood from his eyes. Everything was black and burning. He found his bandanna and pressed it hard against his forehead to stanch the flow of blood. Only then did he try blinking his eyes clear. Slowly, he saw the moonlit countryside around him. The blackness caused by the blood in his eyes faded and Slocum began worrying why the sniper hadn't come after him.

A few yards away his Appaloosa stood quietly, tossing its head and looking to him for guidance. Slocum wanted to go to the horse but held back.

That might be the trap. The bushwhacker might be waiting to see if he got up and tried to ride on out. Slocum slipped his Colt Navy from its holster and worked his way around the rock. He dropped flat on his belly and tried to figure out where the gunman had been.

He thought he saw the momentary glint of moonlight off a rifle barrel but couldn't be sure. Slocum tied his bandanna around his head to keep the blood from pouring down into his eyes again, then got his feet under him.

He took his hat and sent it sailing toward his horse. Response was instant. The back shooter in the rocks above him rose, aimed, and fired. Slocum was blinded by the foot-long tongue of flame belching from the rifle, but he knew where the man trying to kill him hid. Slocum rushed forward, got to the rocks under the sniper, and waited.

Still not seeing too well, Slocum used his other senses. He heard the scraping of boots on rock. The metallic click of a new round being chambered told him this snake still had fangs. And the faint smell of tobacco drifted down to him. His would-be killer was a smoker.

Slocum knew enough about the man now to go after him. The man was careless, rushed his shots, and didn't take enough time to choose his ambush site. Slocum could take him.

Moving like a shadow, Slocum climbed the rock to the sniper's left. He kept low, listening for movement. He struck fast when he thought the bushwhacker was leaving.

"Hey, you!" Slocum shouted, getting to the top of the rock. The sniper had dropped off the right side of the boulder. The man stopped, turned, and stared back up at Slocum. His moment of shock at seeing his target so close gave Slocum the chance to get off a round.

The sniper yelped and dived for cover. Slocum stood for a moment, wondering what had gone wrong. He had the man squarely in his sights, yet he had missed. The shot had felt right. And he hadn't even winged the son of a bitch.

Blinking again, Slocum realized he was seeing double. He had shot at the wrong image. Then he had to dive for cover when two rounds sang past his head. On his belly, Slocum wiggled forward and shoved his six-shooter over the edge. He squeezed off a round, cocked the single-action pistol, and waited.

For a minute he waited. Then two and a third. He knew patience, but he doubted his enemy did. Slocum was right. The bushwhacker got impatient and poked his head out. A quick pull of the trigger sent another round in the sniper's direction.

And again Slocum missed. His hand was shaking and his head felt like a rotted melon, ready to split on the vine. He sank down and tried to keep himself from moaning in pain. Waves rocked through him and made him dizzy.

He came around when he heard the sound of running feet. Slocum scrambled forward and saw a fleeing figure. He tried to make out who it was but couldn't. The darkness and his increasingly blurred vision kept him from identifying his attacker. Slocum lifted his six-shooter and started to fire, then lowered the pistol. There wasn't any need to waste a bullet.

Sliding back down the rock, he hit the ground and almost fell. He was shakier than he had thought. His head wound was caked over but still oozed slightly, but what was going on inside his head bothered him the most.

He whistled and his Appaloosa trotted over to stand obediently. Slocum threw his arms around the strong horse's neck to support himself. When the moment's weakness passed, he swung into the saddle.

The Appaloosa looked back at him, as if asking, "Where do we go now?"

Slocum tried to get his bearings. "We have to find the deed," he said, more to himself than the horse. That was the reason he had ridden out here. He had yet to find the LuLu Belle Mine, much less Charles Macmillan's cabin, the loose floorboard, and the baking soda can with the deed in it.

"That way, that way," Slocum said weakly, turning his horse's head in what he thought was the direction of the mine. The Appaloosa started off at a trot that caused Slocum to pass out for a second. When he came to again, he caught sight of a battered wood signpost.

"We're on the right path," Slocum muttered. "Keep going, keep going, and you'll get us there."

The next thing Slocum realized, the horse was entering Precious. The road broadened and the ramshackle buildings rose on either side. Slocum blinked, wondering how they had gotten back so fast. Then he realized that the sign he had seen sported an arrow pointing in the direction he had ridden.

"I need help," Slocum said, wondering where he was going to find it in Precious. People seemed inclined to offer him jobs here, but he needed a doctor's help. Or someone who could patch him up.

Mrs. Addington's Boardinghouse, read a sign off to his right. It took Slocum a long time to remember why that sounded familiar. Then he remembered Lurene Macmillan's words. She was there. And he needed help.

Slocum slipped from the Appaloosa and staggered along, the horse at his side. He went to the rear of the boardinghouse and sank down to his knees. This wasn't right. He shouldn't get Lurene involved. People would talk and ruin her reputation.

Besides, he didn't know which of the many rooms in the sprawling house was Lurene's.

The Appaloosa neighed loudly and tried to pull away from him. Slocum clung grimly to the reins, not wanting the horse to run off. Without the powerful horse, he would be left afoot and helpless.

"John?" came a soft voice. "Is that you?"

Slocum thought his horse was talking to him. He struggled to his feet and took a step toward the Appaloosa, which was backing away from him.

"Stand still, you varmint," he said. Then his balance went awry again, and Slocum slammed hard into the boardinghouse's wood wall.

"John, you're hurt! Wait a minute. I'll come help you!"

"How are you going to help me?" Slocum asked the Appaloosa. The horse looked at him curiously. Then arms circled him and propelled him toward the boardinghouse.

"What's going on?"

"John, you've been shot!" Lurene's voice came through the fog in his brain. "Don't fight me. You're too strong, even wounded."

Slocum relaxed a mite and let Lurene Macmillan guide him toward the back porch. She tethered his horse, then helped him up the steep steps. He almost collapsed in a chair. Lurene knelt beside him and peeled back the bloody bandanna. She caught her breath.

"That's a nasty wound. Can you tell me what happened?"

"Bushwhacker. On the way to the mine. Never got there, I reckon. Thought I was headed that way but got turned around after he shot me."

"Who was it? Was it one of the claim jumpers?"

"Don't know who. Didn't see him." Slocum's thoughts wandered. Kenny Moore had died with two bullets in his back.

If he hadn't stolen Slocum's duster, he might still be alive. One back shooting had failed. Two had failed now. Slocum wobbled and almost fell out of the chair where he sat.

"I'll get you cleaned up. Don't try leaving, John. You won't get far in your condition."

Slocum wasn't sure if he obeyed out of good sense or just because he couldn't move anymore. Lurene returned with a rag dipped in cool water and laved away the caked blood on his face. She continued to work while Slocum rested. By the time she was finished, he felt better and had a clean bandage circling his head.

"Are you all right, John? You look pale."

"I'm seeing better," Slocum said. His double vision had cleared and the lovely blond snapped into sharp focus. He might have just had his brain shaken up a mite from the bullet rattling past. "Thanks to you, I'm just fine."

He tried standing and found himself in Lurene's arms. He wasn't as strong as he'd thought.

"Rest," Lurene urged. "There's no hurry to go."

"You don't want to be seen with me. It'd ruin your reputation, especially at this time of night. You're a proper lady, and I'm nothing but a drifter."

Slocum heard Lurene's reply as if he stood at the bottom of a well. The world got darker around him, collapsing to a single bright circle. Then even this dancing dot vanished. He remembered the soft sound of her voice long after all vision had fled into shadows. And then even her words disappeared.

Slocum came upright, grabbing for his six-shooter. His hand smashed into a galvanized tub and rang loudly. Soapy water splashed around him, sending waves to and fro over his naked crotch. Slocum blinked hard and saw Lurene at the foot of the wash tub, a damp cloth in her hand.

"You're awake. I do declare, you're quite a handful. I never imagined a man could be so heavy."

"What happened?" Slocum demanded. He sat propped up in a bath tub filled with warm, soapy water. He was all too aware of his nakedness. The waves receded at his middle and revealed more than a young lady ought to see.

He noticed that Lurene was fascinated with the sight. Then it came to him that she must have stripped off his filthy clothing and somehow wrestled him into the tub. She had seen far more than she was watching now just under the surface of the soapy water.

"You needed tending. So, I did it," she said simply.

"You shouldn't have."

"John, you worry too much about my reputation. It is nothing if I allow my brother's death to go unavenged. And there's no way I can deal with those claim jumpers without your help. Now, let me finish washing you. You were a sight!"

She bent over and ran the wash rag up and down Slocum's leg. He saw how the water had splashed out and gotten the bodice of her dress damp. The cloth clung to Lurene's lush body with a tenacity that he appreciated. Her breasts were outlined and he saw taut nipples cresting each succulent mound of flesh.

Lurene glanced down when she saw his interest. She blushed delightfully.

"I need to—"

"You don't need to do anything more than you have," Slocum said. "You're doing just fine." He reached out and took her by the shoulders, pulling her forward. Lurene dropped the wash cloth and turned her face upright to Slocum's.

"You shouldn't. I shouldn't."

He silenced her with a kiss. She didn't try to pull away. If anything, she returned the kiss with more passion than

Slocum had given it. She slipped partially into the tub with him. Water sloshed over the sides as Lurene's skirts spread over Slocum's legs.

"You always take a bath fully dressed?" Slocum asked. Lurene struggled to sit upright, but he didn't let her get away. His fingers worked down the front of her dress, unfastening the buttons.

Lurene tried to get out again, then gave up. She turned around and settled down, sitting on his lap.

Slocum felt himself responding to the lovely blond's nearness. In this position there was only pain waiting for him. His loins churned with need and his manhood stirred.

He quickly stripped off her dress and tossed the soggy clothing aside onto a pile of hay. For the first time he saw that they were in a barn. His Appaloosa stood in a stall a few feet away, watching with white-rimmed eyes. Slocum shot the horse a quick wink and then went back to working on Lurene's clothing.

"These danged things are beyond me," he said, trying to get her free of her frilly undergarments.

Lurene laughed in delight. She arched her back and began wiggling. This let Slocum's thick shaft rise under the woman, and she knew it when she reached under her behind to slide the damp linen garments off.

"What did I find? Is this something that needs my full attention?" she teased.

"Reckon it is," Slocum said. He sat up a little straighter in the tub when Lurene settled back down in his lap. His arms circled her body. The hands came to rest over her firm, full breasts. Slocum cupped her breasts and squeezed down gently.

Lurene sighed in delight and wiggled her behind around, sloshing more water from the tub. She got her legs into the small tub and levered herself up just enough.

Slocum felt her fingers stroking his long shaft. Electric surges passed down into his loins. Then he caressed the woman's thighs and moved around to the blond triangle nestled between her legs.

He stroked over the slickened flesh he found there. Lurene sobbed with joy and shook all over. And Slocum gulped. The woman's fingers tightened around him as she lowered herself.

"There, oh, yes, there!" she sobbed out. Lurene sank down and Slocum's shaft vanished into her seething interior. For a moment they sat still, both savoring the sensations rippling through them. Lurene began moving slowly, turning from side to side.

Slocum gulped and tried not to lose control. The movements of Lurene's hips were small, subtle, and completely arousing. The passions mounted in her body that were already building in Slocum's. She began lifting her hips up and dropping back to Slocum's lap, driving his rigid length far into her body.

"Oh, yes, yes!" she gasped out. "I never felt anything like this before!"

Slocum reached around and stroked her thighs, her heaving belly, the gently bouncing mounds of her breasts. He caught the coppery buttons atop the breasts between thumbs and forefingers and began pinching harder and harder.

Every time he increased the pressure, Lurene rose and fell faster. She was gasping and moaning by the time her body went stiff and she shook all over like a leaf fluttering in a high wind. Then she sank back down, Slocum still firmly lodged within her.

"Don't stop now," Slocum whispered in her ear, nibbling a bit. He kissed her shoulders and neck and kept up his assault on her heavy breasts. "I'm in pain enough without you leaving me like this!"

"Does this help?" Lurene asked. Her fingers found the tight bag holding his balls. She began massaging softly, moving up and down just enough to push Slocum over the edge. He tried to bury himself deeply in the woman but her weight and the tightness of the bathtub prevented it. He had to be content to accept whatever the blond gave.

But Slocum wasn't going to complain. In his condition, this was more than he had any right to expect.

"Enough," he said happily, when he had spent. Slocum settled back in the tub. The water had turned cool around him, but he hardly noticed. "That was about the best ever, Lurene."

"I enjoyed it, too," she said almost shyly. The woman got out of the tub. From where Slocum sat, this was almost as enjoyable as their lovemaking. Naked, she moved to get a towel and dry herself off. Slocum boldly watched, although Lurene was obviously uneasy. She smiled shyly but didn't turn to keep her private parts hidden from him.

"You are a brazen man, aren't you, John?" she asked as she climbed back into her linen undergarments.

"Let's just say I enjoy beauty wherever I find it." Slocum tried to straighten his leg and found he couldn't. He used both hands to pull his right leg out. It hadn't given him any trouble until now. The leg had healed well enough, but it needed some more pampering, at least for a while.

"How is your head?" Lurene asked. She came over and examined the shallow groove across Slocum's forehead. Her gentle fingers caused a slight pain that went away quickly.

"I'm doing fine," Slocum said, getting out of the tub. "But somebody's going to pay for what they did to me."

With his life, he silently added.

5

"Where are you going, John?" Lurene Macmillan asked. "You're in no condition to breeze on out of here. You need to rest." It was hard for Slocum to think of her as the mothering type after being with her in the bathtub, but that was the way she sounded.

"I didn't hear any complaints from you about my condition a while back," Slocum said, strapping on his cross-draw holster. He made sure the Colt Navy rode easy on his left hip, then drew it and began reloading the spent chambers. He didn't want to find the bushwhacker and have a half-empty pistol.

Lurene blushed and started to speak, only to get too embarrassed to continue. Slocum found her demure and altogether appealing. But she had hired him to do a job, and he intended to finish it, even if it meant men died.

He had started to the LuLu Belle Mine because she had offered him half the claim. Now it had turned more personal. He enjoyed the time spent with Lurene in the washtub, but that wasn't what drove Slocum now. Someone had tried to dry-gulch him, and he wasn't going to let that snake get away with it.

"You ought to go to the marshal. I know he refused to help me before, but this time—"

"Marshal Kent will refuse again. He's got trouble aplenty right here in Precious." Slocum smiled crookedly. He might just take the marshal up on his offer to be a deputy. That'd make investigating the claim jumpers at Macmillan's mine a whale of a lot easier. But even as the idea crossed his mind, Slocum discarded it. He couldn't see himself wearing a badge, no matter what.

"I've heard stories of a vigilance committee being formed. I'm not sure what that means, but they might aid us." Lurene Macmillan was an innocent and had no notion of what a bunch of vigilantes might do, once turned loose on a crime.

"I'd as soon not get them involved," Slocum said gently. There was no reason to disillusion the young woman. If the vigilantes were brought in, they might end up hanging anyone who got in their way. "I can handle any trouble that comes up." He slid the Colt back into its holster. He felt fine now, ready to whip his weight in wildcats.

"I'm worried, John. This isn't right, sending you out alone. Maybe we can find someone else to help you." She was earnest, but Slocum wasn't going to argue the point with her. He rode alone or he didn't go out at all. He had found damned few men he trusted to stand at his back, and even fewer he would want to cover it in a showdown.

"If worrying is what you do best, then do it," he told her. "I'll see to the mine." He saw that his Appaloosa had got its fill of hay, watered the horse, then mounted. Lurene ought to have taken off the saddle and other gear, but she was inexperienced and the horse was forgiving enough, now that it had been fed.

Slocum rode out and was startled to see the sun poking over the mountains. He and Lurene had spent longer in the bathtub than he had thought—and he had been unconscious too long. He touched the bandage on his forehead, winced, and then stripped it off. There was no need to advertise how close he had come to getting his head blown off.

He pulled his Stetson down to cover the shallow groove on his forehead as he rode through town. Precious was alive now and commerce was booming. Men pulled in heavy cartloads of ore for assay and smelting. Slocum thought he saw a stamping mill in the valley a mile or two off. The entire Idaho Territory was booming, and it was all because of the gold and silver being ripped from thick veins of ore under the mountains.

Slocum wanted a part of it. Even if the LuLu Belle wasn't knee-deep in gold, Lurene's brother had made a living out of it. That meant it would sell for a decent price. A few hundred dollars would get Slocum a long way from here— after he settled scores with an unknown back shooter.

He rode out of Precious and urged the Appaloosa to a quick trot. He was anxious to reach the mine and see if the claim jumpers were still there. Lurene had assumed they were going to stay and had never thought that her brother might have enemies. Whoever had killed Charles Macmillan might have been content with burying him six feet under and simply walked away from the mine.

If that was the case, Slocum had to look harder for whomever had tried to kill him. It was easy to think that the claim jumpers were also responsible for gunning him down. As he rode, he frowned, in deep thought. That still didn't go far enough in telling him who had shot Kenny Moore in the back and ruined a perfectly good duster.

A cairn of rock and a wooden sign with LuLu Belle lettered on it showed the way to Charles Macmillan's claim. Slocum studied the road and saw confused tracks. The thin, deep grooves from the buckboard wheels showed that Lurene had passed this way and returned. At least two horses had also come this way within the past few hours.

Slocum urged his horse off the double-rutted road and circled, thinking to come up on the mine from down the valley. He found the narrow, rocky draw prevented it. No matter how he rode along the valley, he would be seen from halfway up the hillside. Tailings dribbled from the mouth of the mine and a tumbledown shack stood a few yards away.

He could wait until dark and sneak in, or he could be bold about it. Slocum chose the latter course of action. He got back on the road and went directly to the mouth of the LuLu Belle Mine. Two horses were tethered near the cabin.

Slocum turned when he heard echoes from deep within the mine. The horses' owners were returning. He considered simply gunning them down as they came out, then discarded the notion. He wasn't sure he trusted Lurene's version of what had happened here. He wasn't even sure she had a brother, for all that.

"Howdy, mister," greeted a well-dressed man as he emerged from the mine shaft. "What brings you up to our claim?"

"You the owner?" Slocum asked. The man's silk cravat was held in place with a large diamond stickpin that must have set him back a good hundred dollars. Well-shined boots had a thin coating of dust on them, showing little hard work was done while wearing them. The broadcloth coat was similarly dirty, but not grimy as it would be if anyone was foolish enough to work in a mine wearing it.

A second man appeared behind the fop. This man wore canvas pants, a broadcloth shirt, and a six-shooter at his side that looked well-used. The man had a scar running across his left cheek that gave him the look of a perpetual grin. But there was no amusement in the cold, dark eyes glaring at Slocum.

"Who is this owlhoot, Mr. Farnsworth?" the second man asked.

"I'm trying to find that out, Stan." The dandy turned back to Slocum and said, "My assistant asks a good question. Who are you and what do you want? We're a way off the main road and well nigh an hour's ride outside Precious."

"Came looking for a friend of mine by the name of Charles Macmillan. You gents wouldn't happen to know where I could find him, would you?" Slocum watched their reactions carefully.

The well-dressed man's face never changed. He would be a hell of a poker player. The rougher man's lips curled into a sneer that Slocum took to mean they did know Charles Macmillan.

"He sold this claim to me a few weeks back. I can't say where he might be now, Mister—?" The dandy left the sentence dangling, urging Slocum to complete it.

"Slocum's my name, Mr. Farnsworth," he answered. "You don't look to be a hard miner. Either of you."

"I'm a lawyer over in Coeur d'Alene and have considerable interest in local real estate, especially developed mining properties," Farnsworth said in an oily tone, as if he had practiced his speech in front of a mirror. "This is my assistant, Stanton Howe. Are you interested in buying a mine or just in finding the previous owner?"

"A little of both," Slocum lied. "I was talking to him about buying part interest in the LuLu Belle."

"You don't look like no miner," Howe accused.

"I have an interest in real estate, especially developed mining properties," Slocum said, parroting what Farnsworth had just said. This caused Howe to push past his boss. His hand went for his gun.

Slocum was faster. He dragged his Colt Navy from its holster, cocked it, and had it aimed at Howe before the man cleared leather.

"You looking to sell your interest in this mine?" Slocum asked, as if he hadn't drawn down on Howe and was covering him.

Farnsworth motioned for his gunman to back off. Howe did so, with ill-concealed anger.

"I am always open to offers for my property. That's how I make money. What had you offered the former owner for a share in this mine?"

"I told Macmillan that depended on what I found here. I need to get some ore and run assay on it. And I have to be sure whoever's selling has clear title. I wouldn't want to be accused of being a claim jumper." Again Slocum watched the men's reaction.

Stan Howe almost went for his six-shooter again, but Slocum still had his out and resting easily on his left leg. All it would take was a small jerk to get the Colt Navy up and firing. Farnsworth took the taunt with more grace.

"That's to be expected. Rumors abound of men willing to kill others to steal their claims. Most aren't true, of course, but they make for good tales to spin around a campfire, don't they, Mr. Slocum?" Farnsworth was taking his measure of Slocum, even as Slocum tried to figure how far the lawyer might go.

He wasn't sure what Farnsworth thought of him, but Slocum had already formed his opinion of Farnsworth. He vowed never to shake hands with the man without counting his fingers afterward.

"Mind if I look around?" Slocum asked. He watched Howe to see if the man was likely to kill him if he turned his back, even for an instant. Slocum decided Howe was more likely to do that than face him. Stanton Howe had the look of a coward and a killer.

"Help yourself. My assistant and I were just on our way out."

"What's the assay run on this mine?" Slocum asked, dismounting. He kept the Appaloosa between him and Howe. He faced Farnsworth and found the man to be almost six inches shorter. The lawyer moved to stand on a pile of rock to increase his height so he could look Slocum squarely in the eye.

"Why don't you get some ore from the LuLu Belle and check it for yourself?" suggested Farnsworth. "That way, you'll know everything's on the up and up." Farnsworth motioned to his gunman. Howe growled deep in his throat and followed his boss to the horses tethered nearby.

Slocum was puzzled. He couldn't believe a claim jumper would let his poke around on his own. What if he uncovered Charles Macmillan's body and found evidence of foul play? From all Lurene had said, her brother hadn't been killed in a fair fight.

The lawyer and gunman rode away. When they reached the foot of the hill, Slocum went to the cabin and entered. The interior had been completely stripped. There was no indication anyone had lived here, much less Lurene's brother. She had told him the baking soda tin was near the stove. There wasn't any stove.

Slocum dropped to his hands and knees and looked over the floor for signs that nails had been pulled loose on any of the boards. A discolored area showed where a stove might have stood, but there wasn't any smoke hole in the roof under it. He pried up a few boards and peered down. All he saw was solid rock.

Disgusted, Slocum gave up his search and went outside into the warm Idaho sunlight. He looked around the tailings and found a few pieces of ore good enough for an assay. Like most miners, Charles Macmillan was interested only in the best pieces of ore from his mine. He discarded chunks that might be marginal, even if they carried enough gold in them to keep most men happy for a night's drinking.

Slocum took out his knife and scraped at the gold slivers he found in the ore. Fool's gold was bright, shiny, and had sharp faces on each crystal. What he found was shiny enough, but the crystalline faces were rounded, weathered. He scraped away a bit and smiled. "Gold," he said to himself. "This mine *is* a good one."

Slocum looked around again, having the feeling of someone looking over his shoulder. He didn't see anyone.

He tucked a piece of the ore into his pocket. All an assayer needed was a few grams of ore to do a good analysis. Slocum had watched the process often enough to be able to do it himself if he had the equipment. But he didn't have the ceramic crucibles or the kiln needed to melt the rock or any of the chemicals required to dissolve the gold. he wasn't even sure where he would get mercury for a quick field check on how good the ore was.

Slocum poked around, looking at the twin rails coming from the depths of the mine. They were rusted. Charles Macmillan might have taken them from another, older mine. It wasn't unusual for a miner to find played out or worthless mines and steal whatever equipment he could drag off. A tipped-over ore cart showed that Macmillan had pulled it out by himself. He hadn't even used a mule or goat.

One-man operations were both dangerous and incredibly hard to work. Slocum figured Charles Macmillan would go inside, single jack his holes, plant his dynamite, and blow out the face in the mine, then muck the rubble himself. Day after day, week after week, it was lonely work and normally unrewarding.

Slocum touched the ore sample in his pocket. If Macmillan discarded ore with obvious gold in it, the LuLu Belle Mine might be worth a whale of a lot more than it appeared. Certainly it was valuable enough for claim jumpers to have killed the man.

All that bothered Slocum was how open the lawyer seemed. He doubted Farnsworth was an innocent purchaser from the claim jumpers. He was responsible, he and his hired gun, Stanton Howe. But Slocum worried that Lurene wasn't telling him everything. The lawyer had done a good job of removing any sign that a man named Charles Macmillan had ever been here.

And if he pored over the land records, Slocum was sure he'd find no trace of any claim laid by Lurene's brother. Lawyers had a way of doctoring records better than anyone else. They knew where the skeletons were hidden and how to bribe and blackmail and make it all look legal. Slocum wished he had found the original claim to the mine.

Slocum stopped at the mouth of the mine and looked around again, the hairs on the back of his neck rising. He touched the ebony handle of his Colt Navy but saw no obvious target. For all he could tell, he was alone on the mountainside. But the feeling of being watched still dogged him.

"Getting spooked after last night," he muttered. Slocum went into the mine's mouth and examined the timbers. If Charles Macmillan had stolen old equipment from other mines, he might have done the same for the timbers shoring the ribs and back of the mine. Slocum was pleased to see that the miner had used new timber.

"Looks secure," he said to himself. He paused and looked out the mouth before going inside a few yards. Slocum found a carbide lamp and sloshed the water around inside. He smiled. He wouldn't have to go scare up a few swigs of water for the light. He saw the box of carbide pellets nearby. He dropped a pebble into the chamber, got the water moving over it, and produced a bright, white light.

Slocum had worked in mines where the only light came from candles. This was much better, not giving off smoke or flickering light that could hide danger in shifting shadows.

He walked down the shaft, noting how few pockets of ore had been dug out along the way. He turned and looked behind him. The single opening shone brightly with the sunlight beyond.

"Just my luck," Slocum grumbled to himself. "He dug an adit."

Uneasy but not unduly worried that there was only the single opening, Slocum went farther into the mine. He found where larger chunks of ore had been mined, indicating veins running off the main lode. Slocum took a few samples here and there and started deeper, wanting to find the last place Charles Macmillan had worked.

Something stopped him. He turned and looked back toward the tiny opening. A dark figure crossed the opening, just for an instant. Slocum frowned. Was it only his imagination or was someone outside?

He gave up his search for the most recent blasting and digging and started back for the mouth of the mine.

"Hey!" Slocum shouted. His hand flashed for his Colt Navy, but he was too slow. He *had* seen someone outside. And he also saw the flare of a length of black miner's fuse being lit.

Slocum pounded forward, trying to get out of the mine. Never had he run faster—but to no avail.

The explosion picked him up and tossed him back into the mine. Dust billowed and choked him, and he no longer saw the bright opening filled with spring. He was trapped in the mine!

6

Slocum lay flat on his back, staring up at rock threatening to come tumbling down on top of him. He tried to move but couldn't. He coughed and spat dirt and blood, then struggled to sit up. For a moment he wondered what was wrong.

The carbide light still burned and showed the tumble of rock blocking the way out of the adit. That bothered him, but there was something else. His head hurt like an Indian had scalped him. Slocum touched his forehead and saw that the shallow groove had opened again and was trickling blood down his face. He took off his bandanna and fastened it around his head, sorry now that he hadn't left Lurene's clean white bandage in place.

But there was something else troubling him. Then it came to him. He couldn't hear the hiss of the carbide lamp. He picked up a rock and smashed it down into another rock. Nothing. No sound. He was deaf as a post from the roar of the dynamite that closed the mine.

For some reason, this bothered him more than the idea of being trapped in the mine.

Only when his ears began to ring and he heard the faint

creaking of mine timbers and the distant fall of rock deeper in the mine did he know real fear. Trapped. He was trapped in the mine and didn't see any way of ever digging out.

Slocum went to the rock fall and crawled to the top of the tunnel. He pawed at the rock, hoping to winnow through the larger rock and poke out a hole that would let him see daylight. Twenty minutes of hot, sweaty work convinced him he would never get through the thick plug in the tunnel. Whoever had set the charge had brought down most of the mine's back, efficiently trapping him.

Trapped. Trapped!

Slocum fought down rising panic. He sat on his haunches and stared at the sputtering carbide light. The water inside was running low. When it was used up by the carbide crystalline, he would be completely in the dark. If that happened, he would have no chance at all of escaping.

Turning from the fall in the tunnel's mouth, Slocum worked his way deeper into the mine. He hoped to find a stope running upward. Charles Macmillan might have found a vein running away and worked it. If he had, there might be only a few feet from the top of the stope to freedom. Walking around above a mining area was dangerous because of the thin layers of rock left between stope and surface.

He found nothing. Despair growing, Slocum walked faster, and his haste almost killed him.

He tripped, fell to his knees, and then tumbled downward into a pit. Rocks cut at him as he pitched forward. And then he found himself gasping for breath. Cold water closed around him. Slocum flailed around and found an outjutting of rock. Fingers grasping this simple sanctuary, Slocum pulled himself up and out of the water.

He spat and took a moment to regain his strength. Far above him he saw the shining light from the lantern. Slocum shook himself and then began kicking and struggling to get his feet under him. Slippery slime made it hard going but Slocum got onto a narrow ledge. For a few minutes, he just sat and wondered what was going to happen to him.

Then Slocum began getting mad. Someone had back shot Kenny Moore because the sneak thief had stolen Slocum's duster. On his way to the LuLu Belle Mine, a bushwhacker had tried to gun him down. Now he was sealed in a mine by someone who had deliberately set a dynamite charge.

"You're dead, Farnsworth," Slocum vowed, anger mounting even more. He realized the oily lawyer wasn't one who had actually planted the dynamite. He would leave dirty work like that to his henchman. Stanton Howe was added to his list of people to get even with.

Anger burning brighter by the second, Slocum began climbing the wall of the shaft. He saw that this was a natural pit, not one Charles Macmillan had dug. Miners followed ore lodes vertically in drifts, not paying a whole lot of attention to direction. If they saw a vein of ore going vertically, they always dug up. It was easier to let the rock fall than to use a winch and bucket to pull it up from the bottom of a pit such as Slocum had tumbled into.

"Natural pit," Slocum grumbled to himself as he came to the rim. Fingers bleeding from the sharp rocks, he pulled himself up and over the rim and lay in the dirt, gasping for breath. It seemed to him the air was turning foul. That meant Macmillan had cut only the single opening. There weren't any stopes opening to the daylight.

He thought of the vast prairies and endless stretches of mountains he had come to love. The Bitterroot Mountains would be lost to him forever. Never again would he ride along, wind in his face, the feeling of freedom moving him from town to town.

"Get out of here," he grumbled to himself. "There's got to be a way. There must be." Slocum heaved himself to his feet, glad the lantern was still glowing. He turned down the intensity to make the carbide last, then skirted the pit.

Charles Macmillan hadn't laid ore cart tracks here. That made Slocum think the miner had been working nearby. He cast the light up at the back, hoping to see the shaft he had fallen into extend upward. It didn't. He walked around the shaft with the promised watery grave at the bottom and found the mine's face within a few paces.

Macmillan had cut a dozen bore holes. Four center holes, six cutter holes, and then the miner had started marking the long line of lifter holes at the bottom. He had never finished jacking them.

Slocum touched the face and saw where Lurene's brother had found a new vein of ore. Using his knife, Slocum scraped off a few pieces of ore and tucked them into his vest pocket, too. Then he stopped and thought hard.

He was missing something. It took several seconds for him to realize what it was.

"Here it is," Slocum said, smiling crookedly. To one side of the face were a dozen sticks of dynamite, laid out and waiting to be thrust into the bore holes Charles Macmillan had jacked into the rock.

Slocum gingerly examined the dynamite. A few sticks were sweating. He pushed them aside, not wanting to touch the nitroglycerin-leaking sticks. Charles Macmillan had carelessly stored several dozen blasting caps next to the dynamite. Slocum carefully picked up a half dozen of the small fulminate of mercury caps. Adding to this, he picked up six sticks of dynamite, wondering if he could blast his way back through the rock fall blocking the mouth of the mine.

Somehow, he doubted it. The rumble had deafened him for

a few minutes. That meant tons and tons of rock had come down. He was more likely to bury himself than he was to blow his way clear. There had to be another way out, now that he had the means.

Picking up a ten-foot length of miner's fuse, Slocum worked his way back along the mine, hunting for any spot where the walls might be weak enough to blow through. He came back to the pit he had taken the fall into, then smiled. He knew how miners worked. They blasted upward so the rock would fall past them. Slocum's problem was being in a mine shaft with a single entrance and exit.

But if he blasted over the pit, the rock would go into the water at the bottom. This would take care of tons of rock and the water at the bottom would keep dust from rising to choke him.

Slocum climbed up and looked at the rock above the pit. There were natural crevices hinting that the mountain's surface might not be too far above. He tried to sniff any hint of fresh air in the cracks but failed. He would have to set the charges and hope for the best.

Slocum had worked as a powder monkey and knew how to plant charges. He would have preferred to bore a few holes into the rock for maximum effect, but the air was getting stuffier by the minute. He didn't think he had much time left. Placing six sticks of dynamite, he inserted the blasting caps, then cut a spitter fuse to set off the sticks in a staggered blast.

Slocum jumped back down and looked at his handiwork. He'd only have one chance. The explosion would fill the entire tunnel with so much smoke and dust he'd suffocate in a few minutes. If he succeeded, he'd blow a hole all the way to the top of the mountain. Slocum sucked in his breath, realizing it might be his last, then lit the fuse.

The gunpowder inside the miner's fuse sputtered and caught. A long tail of sparks shot out, then vanished as the fuse burned along the length at one foot per minute. Slocum backed off, then ran toward what had been the mouth of the tunnel.

The blast caught him by surprise. A giant hand lifted him and slammed him hard against the rock fall. He lay, dazed and shaken. It finally occurred to him that the dust that had billowed around him carried a new quality—light.

Sneezing and coughing, he worked his way back along the rubble-strewn mine until he came to the pit. It was half filled with the rock that had fallen from his blast.

Above him shone the brilliant springtime Idaho sun.

"I did it!" he crowed. Slocum wasted no time working his way into the chimney he had blasted through the mountain. The cracks in the rock must have reached the surface for the blast to have cleared it out all the way. Slocum cut himself several times on sharp-edged rock, but he didn't mind. The circle of light above him promised freedom, and he labored to reach it.

It took almost a half hour to make his way up the jagged chimney, but he finally tumbled out onto the mountainside, high above the mine entrance. Slocum sat up and looked around. Realization came slowly that the mine below him wasn't the LuLu Belle. He had emerged on the far side of the mountain.

He sat in the warm sunlight and studied the mine, trying to figure out what struck him as wrong.

"Not much in the way of tailings," he decided. The mine looked to be well established. A large cabin set halfway down the mountain had been lived in for some time. Two wrecked ore carts were rusting outside, showing some activity in the mine. But the tailings were sparse.

Slocum checked his Colt Navy to be sure it was in good working condition. The cylinder spun easily and the hammer came back without any telltale gritting in its mechanism.

He replaced his gun and made his way down the hillside to the mine, wondering who worked it. Perhaps the mine's owner could answer a few questions that might give him some much-needed information about the LuLu Belle Mine. He didn't doubt Lurene's assertion that Charles Macmillan had owned it. Anything Farnsworth or his hired gun said was instantly suspect, but questions still haunted him.

What had become of Charles Macmillan's body? There was little sign that Lurene's brother or anyone else had ever lived in the cabin at the mine. No stove, no belongings, nothing. He knew Farnsworth would want to erase all evidence of a previous tenant if there had been foul play, but he had worked damned fast.

Slocum slipped down the rest of the way and came to a stop beside the mouth of the mine. He peered in, listening hard for any hint of activity. He was still deafened from the second dynamite blast, but Slocum didn't think there was anyone working this mine right now. From the condition of the track, ore carts seldom went in or out.

He looked around and saw a poorly painted wood sign telling him this was the Phantom Mine. That meant nothing to Slocum. But whoever lived here must be in the cabin.

Slocum walked downhill to the cabin along an ill-defined path, more proof that the Phantom wasn't being actively worked. He stopped outside the door and called, "Hello. Anybody home?"

No answer.

Slocum circled the cabin and saw a thin column of black smoke coming from the stovepipe sticking out the back wall. He went to a window and tried to see inside. The dirty pane prevented him from telling if anyone was in the cabin.

He returned to the front and called out again. Then he knocked. Only then did Slocum cautiously open the door and peer inside. He sucked in his breath at what he found.

Slocum had been in fancy hotels in Denver and San Francisco and New Orleans. Seldom had he seen such opulence. A heavy rug on the floor deadened his footfalls as he entered to look around. Heavy carved wood furniture lined the walls. A four-poster bed stood to the far side of the large cabin. Gilded mirrors hung on the walls and several oil paintings decorated the other bare spots.

There were even two stoves inside the cabin. The one at the far side of the cabin vented through the wall; Slocum had seen it from outside. Another stove stood just inside the door but hadn't been vented yet. With both potbellied stoves running, the interior of the cabin would hold back even the fiercest Idaho winter.

He let out a low whistle. This was no line shack inhabited by a hard rock miner grubbing in the ground just to stay alive. Hundreds of dollars, maybe thousands, had been spent on everything in the cabin. Slocum walked to a desk and poked through the papers. Several were emblazoned with the words Phantom Mine, but he couldn't figure out what the letters were about. Two assay reports showed the mine to be fabulously rich, though.

Slocum scratched his head. Maybe there was another Phantom Mine. With an assay showing six ounces of gold per ton, there ought to be a dozen miners up the hill dragging out ore. The lack of tailings showed how little work was being done.

A distant gunshot caught his attention. Slocum walked back to the door and looked around. Farther down the hill he saw a white cloud of gunsmoke. He left the cabin, closing the door behind him. From a vantage point atop a large rock, Slocum shielded his eyes with his hand and tried to see who was doing the shooting—and why.

A second report echoed up to him. Only then did Slocum locate the gunman.

The tall, thin figure hardly cast a shadow. Slocum smiled crookedly when he recognized the man who had played against him in the poker game at the Gold Tooth Saloon.

"Carson," he muttered. "So this is your mine."

Another gunshot and the sound of a bullet ricocheting into the distance made Slocum squint. He finally decided the miner was doing some target practice and murdering empty tin cans. The miner went and set up another rail filled with cans, walked back ten paces, and started firing again. Carson was a terrible shot, scaring the cans more than hitting them.

Slocum shrugged this off. No matter how bad a shot Carson was, and most miners didn't even bother to wear a six-shooter, he had hit it big with the Phantom. The lavish furniture and other trappings inside the cabin proved that. Hell, Carson even had two potbellied stoves. That was the height of luxury in a place like Precious, Idaho.

There wasn't much he had to say to the skeletal miner, so Slocum jumped down from the rock and looked for a way around the mountain that wouldn't take him past Carson. He saw a faint trail leading up and to the west. Slocum took off, noting that the trail looked to be better used than the one up to the mouth of the Phantom Mine.

As he trudged along, Slocum reveled in the rush of fresh, clean mountain air into his lungs. He didn't even mind the times he sneezed from all the blooming flowers. Only an hour earlier, he hadn't been sure he would ever see daylight again.

Slocum became more cautious as he came around the mountain and neared the LuLu Belle Mine. Farnsworth had set the charge. He was the only one who had anything to gain by killing Slocum, and only he and Howe had known Slocum was inside the mine. It had been foolish to enter without being sure they had really ridden off, but he hadn't thought they would ruin their investment by sealing him in.

That meant his death counted for more than the gold they might mine from the LuLu Belle.

Three times someone had tried to kill him since he'd come to Precious. There wouldn't be a fourth attempt.

Slocum slipped his six-shooter from its holster and crouched down to study the area around Charles Macmillan's ramshackle cabin. It was almost pathetic, compared to Carson's, but Slocum knew this was closer to the way miners really lived. How Carson had become so rich didn't matter as much as gunning down the men who had tried to back shoot and dynamite him.

Slocum waited for almost ten minutes but saw no movement around the mouth of the mine. He worked his way down the hillside and came out just above the dynamited entrance. Dust and rock trailed out from the explosion. Someone had been expert in setting the charge. The timbers supporting the mine's roof were still intact. Although it would take long weeks of work to reopen the LuLu Belle, it could be done.

He heard a horse neighing and went to investigate. To his surprise, Slocum saw his Appaloosa pawing the ground impatiently and trying to pull free of where he had tethered the animal.

"I'll be damned," he said, walking to the horse. He was wary of an ambush, then pushed the notion from his mind. Whoever had tried to seal him in the mine shaft thought he was dead. They wouldn't be trying to ambush him.

Slocum mounted and rode back to Precious, growing madder by the minute. Somebody was going to pay. With his life.

7

Tired, bruised, dirty, and still wet from falling into the pit, Slocum rode back into Precious. It seemed every time he returned to the town, he was in worse shape than when he left. But this time he toyed with the idea of not stopping.

It would be easy enough for him to keep riding after all that had happened to him. He hadn't intended to spend any time in this small mining town, and hadn't even known it was here until he had rescued Lurene Macmillan and the stagecoach's cargo of gold. There wasn't anything for him here. All he had wanted was to rob their stagecoach and get away with a few hundred dollars in gold, but things had changed.

And he wasn't going to just ride off. Not after what had happened to him in the LuLu Belle. His anger smoldered and threatened to flare up like a lightning-strike forest fire. He owed Farnsworth more than he could ever repay. He might kill the shyster lawyer, but that would be little enough.

The more Slocum thought on it, the more he believed Farnsworth was responsible for his other problems. The lawyer and his hired gun had done well covering their tracks at the LuLu Belle. No sign of Charles Macmillan remained, making their claim jumping successful. But Slocum believed that Lurene's brother had owned the mine and that she had been there when he had been murdered.

Farnsworth must have ordered Stanton Howe to do the dirty work. Howe was responsible for lighting the fuse that brought down the tons of rock that almost killed Slocum. And Slocum had come to think that Howe was also responsible for trying to bushwhack him when he had ridden out to the mine the night before.

All that didn't fit into this neat picture was Kenny Moore. Slocum hadn't even met Farnsworth or Howe when the sneak thief was gunned down. He had to admit that Moore might have angered someone else in Precious. Boomtowns were infamous for hardworking, hard-drinking men and their hair-trigger tempers. The thief might have stolen one item too many and another of the miners had caught up with him.

"How many of them wear six-shooters?" Slocum muttered. Few miners wore pistols because there was so little need. They worked underground twelve hours a day and when they drank, their idea of fun was getting staggering drunk, not shooting up a saloon. That was more what a cowboy would do after a six-week cattle drive.

Slocum smiled a little remembering the towns he had rampaged in after a long cattle drive. Shooting out windows and riding through saloons somehow let off the steam that built week after weeks on the trail. But the pressures on a miner were different. They didn't use guns as much as they did their fists, taking satisfaction in hitting rather than shooting.

So why did Kenny Moore die?

Slocum pushed it from his mind. He was sure of Farnsworth and Howe and their guilt. After he took care of them, he'd worry about who had ventilated his perfectly good duster while Moore was wearing it.

Riding past Mrs. Addington's Boardinghouse convinced Slocum he shouldn't stop to inquire after Lurene. Women bustled about on the front porch, having finished their noon meal. None of the young ladies he saw would permit him to speak to Lurene out of simple good taste. Slocum touched his vest pocket and found the soggy wad of greenbacks he had won in the poker game. He still had a goodly poke.

He dismounted and led his horse toward a livery. The Appaloosa had been a reliable mount throughout this whole wretched affair, and Slocum wanted the horse tended to properly. He paid the hostler a dollar to feed and curry the horse, then found himself a barber shop sandwiched between a bookstore and a funeral parlor. The bath couldn't compare to the one Lurene had given him the night before, but Slocum didn't complain. He had his clothes washed out, and when he finished with a shave, he felt a world better.

Stretching mightily, he looked up and down the main street. Precious was like most boomtowns. The miners were hard at work underground and the only commerce that went on was restocking for their nightly visit.

He pulled the ore samples taken from the LuLu Belle Mine out of his pocket and sauntered across the street to the assayer's office, Klarner and Son, according to the simple sign swinging outside the door. The old man behind the counter whom Slocum took to be Klarner was busy running ore samples through a chipmunk tooth grinder. He looked up and peered at Slocum through thick magnifying lenses that turned his eyes into bloodshot saucers.

"What can I do for you, mister?" the assayer asked. Klarner had sized up Slocum in a single glance and decided his customer didn't look like a new prospector come to ask after a new claim.

"I need these assayed as soon as you can get to them," Slocum said, dropping four samples to the desk. The assayer peered at Slocum curiously, picked up the rock, and shrugged.

"Take a week or more. I'm busier than a starving cat in a mouse factory."

"Could I run my own tests?"

"No need. Got an assistant around somewhere. He needs the practice, if you're not looking for real accurate work. Where is that worthless kid?" The assayer bellowed for his assistant. A youth of hardly sixteen hurried in. He carried an ax in his hand and was sweating profusely.

"What is it, sir? I was out back chopping wood to fire the kiln."

"Run an assay for this gentleman. He wants it right away."

"But it'd take at least ten hours to get a good reading on any ore."

"I know, son," Slocum cut in. "You don't have to be exact. Just give me a quick and dirty notion of what I've got here."

"Might grind it up and use mercury to form an amalgam," the boy said, looking to the old man for approval. Klarner nodded and went back to his work. The boy took Slocum's samples and began grinding them into powder.

Slocum stood back and watched as the boy worked. For all his youth, he knew his trade. He put the sample in a crucible and heated it with mercury. A gold amalgam formed and was removed from the slag. The boy worked to separate the gold from the mercury and finally came up with tiny gold specks in the bottom of his crucible.

"It looks to be a decent enough sample, sir," the boy said. "See the specks? Might be worth as much as a nickel for these pieces."

"What's it assay to for a ton of ore?" Slocum asked. He wasn't interested in dust. He wanted to know what Lurene's claim was worth—and what Farnsworth was willing to murder for.

"At least two ounces per ton. Maybe three, if you found a good part of the lode," the boy said. "That's not too rich, but it beats worthless rock, like so much of what we see in here." He pointed to a glass-fronted cabinet filled with huge chunks of fool's gold and mica. Slocum took this to be the assayer's rogues' gallery filled with the mistakes of over eager prospectors.

"So the claim would be worth working?"

"It wouldn't make you rich, but it'd be better work than this," the boy said under his breath. Klarner either paid no attention or didn't hear. The old man worked at the kiln to pour out a ceramic crucible brimming with molten slag.

"How much do I owe you?"

"Five dollars!" shouted Klarner. Slocum kept from smiling. Nothing got by the old man, not in his own store. Slocum watched as the boy painfully entered the amount in a large ledger and wrote out a receipt for the money.

As the boy worked, Slocum looked over the other entries. He didn't see any for Charles Macmillan, but he hadn't expected to. Macmillan's claim had been active for several months, and he only saw the most recent assays. He saw several that Farnsworth had ordered. And Slocum surprised himself by looking to see if Carson had brought in any ore from the Phantom Mine.

"You do everybody's assay?" Slocum asked.

"Purt near everyone's," the boy said, carefully blotting the receipt and handing it to Slocum.

"What does the Phantom Mine assay out to? Looks like Carson is making a goodly sum off his work."

"We don't discuss our results," Klarner snapped. Then he shook his head. "Old Enoch Carson is a hard worker. Must be to make what he does off the Phantom."

"Why do you say that? The mine looks to be high grade."

Klarner snorted and went back to his work without another word. The boy's eyes got wide, and Slocum saw he was brimming with gossip about Carson.

"You'd best get back to your chores," Slocum said. "I have what I need."

The boy's face fell as he turned and went out back to resume the hard work of chopping firewood. Slocum bade Klarner good-bye and left the assay shop, then went around back. The boy swung the ax without much conviction. He would rather be working in the shop than outside on such menial chores.

"Mind if I talk a spell?" Slocum asked.

"Talk's cheap," the boy said, wiping his forehead. Slocum saw a second ax nearby. He hefted it and began splitting wood on a stump.

The boy smiled and worked a bit more on his wood.

"What's so strange about the Phantom Mine?" Slocum asked, stacking the wood he'd split on the boy's pile. Talk was cheap but the boy would talk all day if he got a bit of help with his tedious chores. The boy smiled a little more broadly, approving of Slocum's help. He seemed willing to have someone to talk to, also.

"Old Carson has a terrible claim, leastwise it's not too good. The first couple assays were piss poor," the boy said. His eyes widened when he realized he had used bad language. He pulled his shoulders back and stood a little taller when he saw Slocum didn't mind. "Then he brought in some of the best ore in the area. High grade ore. Assayed out at eight ounces a ton."

"So he didn't hit the real motherlode right away," Slocum said. "Is that so unusual?"

"He keeps bringing in ore. Most of it is bad, but some is good. After all this time, I don't think he knows what's good and what is worthless rock." The boy split another log and leaned on the ax. "If I didn't know better, I'd think he was some danged nester who finds rocks in his field and just brings them in on a lark."

"Not a good miner, eh?" Slocum said, digesting the information. From the way Carson lived, it looked like he had struck the richest vein in the entire Bitterroot Mountains.

"There are better," the boy said, turning cautious again.

"What about Farnsworth?"

"The lawyer from Coeur d'Alene?" Contempt dripped from the teenager's words. "He's tryin' to buy up everything in these parts. Don't much care if it's worth spit. He just wants to own it all."

"That guarantees him getting the best," Slocum said.

"Along with the worst. He's got more money than good sense. And he's not above using high-handed tactics, too," the boy said, as if confiding a secret.

"I've run across Stanton Howe."

"He's a killer," the boy said, eyes going wide again. "Heard tell he shot a man in the back over in Billings. And another somewhere along the Milk River."

"Which claims have they taken over using these high-handed tactics?" asked Slocum.

"Can't say. It's not my place."

"What about Charles Macmillan? Do you know him?"

"Macmillan? The name's familiar, but I don't know him. Fact is, I don't know much of anybody since we came to Precious. My pa keeps me real busy with the assayin'. I don't even have time to go to school." He smiled almost shyly. "And the schoolmarm's real pretty, too."

"Maybe your pa figures you can learn all you need being apprenticed to him," Slocum said. He smiled and added, "And he knows how little work you'd get done mooning over that teacher."

The boy laughed. "You might be right. But it would be nice to read something other than books on chemistry and new assay methods."

Slocum split one final log and left the boy. He had traded a few split logs for a passel of information, but Slocum wasn't real sure what it all meant. He hadn't learned anything he hadn't already guessed about Farnsworth. The lawyer saw golden—and silver—opportunity around Precious and was trying to get the best of the mines for his own. There was nothing wrong in that.

Except maybe that he was doing it illegally. Charles Macmillan's body must be somewhere under a pile of rock and that would prove Farnsworth was willing to kill in exchange for a deed to a mine.

Slocum went to the land records office and went through the poorly kept deeds that had been filed. He couldn't find any record that Charles Macmillan had registered the LuLu Belle Mine, but he couldn't find any reason to think that he hadn't. Entire pages were missing from the ledger.

"How do I find if a claim is registered? I'd hate to wander around out there in the hills and stake claim to somebody else's mine."

The clerk looked at him as if he didn't quite understand. Then he shrugged and said, "Hard to do. Not everything's listed."

"Why not?" Slocum held his temper in check. The clerk seemed to be intentionally unswayable when it came to giving out information.

"Those claims were being argued in court and have been entered as evidence." The clerk shrugged this off as if it were business as usual.

"So how do you know what's registered and what's not?"

"There are duplicate records."

"But not here," Slocum pressed.

"That's right. There are copies in Boise, if you want them bad enough."

"Can you get them for me?"

The clerk shook his head and that was all the answer Slocum got. He didn't bother pointing out that Precious didn't even have a judge. Any legal squabbling had to be done elsewhere. That was one reason the vigilance committee had formed so quickly after Moore's murder.

Slocum stepped out into the afternoon sun. It was about time to find Lurene and tell her what he had found—and hadn't found. The lack of a deed to the LuLu Belle was going to be hard to get around. Slocum figured Farnsworth had the land clerk on his payroll, and there were probably others.

He saw Marshal Kent across the street. On impulse, Slocum went to speak with the lawman.

"Afternoon, Marshal," Slocum greeted. Kent's cold gaze told him things weren't going well in Precious. The marshal was tense and, from the way his fingers tapped the butt of his six-gun, looked ready to throw down on any man crossing his path.

"Didn't expect to see you again, Slocum," the marshal said.

"You said you were inclined to think that carpetbagger judges didn't much count."

"Nevertheless, we don't cotton much to killers here." Kent looked up and down the street as if he expected a horde of crazed assassins brandishing six-shooters to come galloping up at any instant.

"Got business," Slocum said. He turned cautious when he saw the marshal's expression. "With Farnsworth. You know him? He's a lawyer over in—"

"Coeur d'Alene," Kent said irritably. "I know Mr. Farnsworth. Who doesn't, in these parts? What's your business with him? We got an understanding, Mr. Farnsworth and me."

Slocum backed off. From the way the marshal spoke, he made it sound as if he was on Farnsworth's payroll. And he might have been. Nobody made a land grab without political and legal backing. From all Slocum had seen, Stan Howe wasn't enough to rely on, if shooting started. Like the boy at the assay office had said, Howe might be good for gunning people down from behind, but there were other chores that needed doing in broad daylight.

A town marshal might be perfect for such doings.

"My business won't take long," Slocum said.

Kent didn't answer. He looked around, a nervous tic making his left cheek jerk and dance around like a blob of fat on a hot skillet. Slocum headed for the Gold Tooth Saloon to wet his whistle. He had never learned the barkeep's name, but the man seemed to be a fountain of information. Slocum needed to learn all he could before suggesting a course of action to Lurene Macmillan.

If he was going up against Farnsworth and his hired gun, that was one thing. Having to fight the marshal was something else. Marshals could call in help from nearby cavalry outposts, if the need arose.

"Howdy, Slocum," greeted the barkeep. "The usual? Or do you want to try some of my fine beer?"

"You've got it brewed already?" Slocum remembered the

block of yeast he had saved from the stagecoach robbers.

"Another batch," the barkeep confided. "Best in all of Precious."

"I've got a nickel if you've got the beer," Slocum said. He was pleased to see that the barkeep served it cold. Ice and snow weren't too far up the mountain slopes. Somehow the chill of ice in beer made it taste just a little better on a hot spring day.

As he drank the beer, a roar sounded behind him. Slocum looked over his shoulder and saw two dozen men crowding into the Gold Tooth. He recognized a few as having been the instigators of the vigilance committee. He paid them scant attention until one of the men swaggered over and put his hand on Slocum's shoulder.

"Thought you'd be halfway to Seattle by now," the man said.

"I like Precious. Thought I'd stay around a bit longer." Slocum turned back to his beer, but the man didn't take his hand off his shoulder. Slocum straightened a mite and turned so that he could get to his six-shooter if the need arose.

From the sudden quiet in the Gold Tooth, he thought that it might be necessary. And he didn't understand what had happened to cause it.

"We got a mission. We got to protect the town since the marshal don't seem able to do it."

"A noble undertaking," Slocum said sarcastically. He knew he ought to defer to the vigilante, but John Slocum didn't grovel to any man, even one with twenty or more guns backing him up.

"I been goin' through the marshal's wanted posters."

Slocum put his beer on the bar and turned. "What's that to me?"

The vigilante pulled out a much-folded, faded wanted

poster and held it up. Slocum couldn't see the picture, but he remembered that Marshal Kent had seen a warrant on him for judge killing. The vigilante looked from the poster to Slocum and back, comparing what he saw.

Slocum got ready to put a bullet in the vigilante's fat gut and then take out as many of the crowd as he could before they cut him down.

8

"What are you saying?" Slocum asked, trying not to betray his need for action. The sooner he started shooting, the more likely he was to plug a few of the men. But something held him back.

"This might be a poster on you," the vigilante said truculently. "The picture's a mite faded, but it's for a stage robber, and you was hangin' around the coach."

Slocum laughed harshly. "I'm no road agent. Go ask Mr. Lucas over at the depot. Or the driver of yesterday's stage. I *stopped* three varmints from holding up the stage." Slocum turned back to his beer, wondering if the bluff would work.

"That's right, Marv. He even got a reward. From Lucas, can you imagine that?" This produced a round of laughter. Slocum had gotten the idea that the agent was a tight-fisted old geezer who was more likely to let his mother starve to death than offer her a bite from his own plate. This seemed to convince everyone of his innocence.

Everyone except the vigilante named Marv.

"I dunno. This looks a lot like him."

"Would I be standing here talking to you if I were a stagecoach robbing owlhoot?" asked Slocum. "Give Marv one of those fine beers," he said, dropping a dime on the bar. The barkeep scooped it up and returned with a sweaty glass of beer.

"That's real neighborly of you," Marv said, tasting the beer. The others with him decided they needed to wet their whistles, too. They crowded close and filled the Gold Tooth with boisterous prattle for almost an hour.

All the while, Slocum kept a sharp eye on Marv and the wanted poster the man had returned to his shirt pocket. Slocum had more than one warrant dogging his heels. If Marv had spent much time in the marshal's office, chances were good he had found one for some crime Slocum couldn't even remember committing.

"We're just tryin' to cut down on the crime here in Precious," Marv told Slocum, getting a little drunker with every mouthful of the strong beer he guzzled. "No hard feelings."

"A shame about Kenny Moore," Slocum said, wondering if the vigilance committee had uncovered anything about the man's killer.

"That's just part of it," Marv allowed. "We got robberies goin' on out on the road. It's gettin' so we can't even ship our gold without fear of it disappearin' into some owlhoot's poke."

"And the marshal ain't no good," chimed in another. This was met with a round of agreement.

"What's Marshal Kent's problem?" Slocum asked, as much to keep the men thinking of matters other than the wanted poster stuffed into in Marv's pocket. Now and again Marv touched it and looked hard at Slocum, his eyes narrowing just a mite. The slip of yellowed paper poked just out of the miner's shirt pocket and mocked Slocum.

"He don't keep the peace, that's what," someone said. This

vague accusation was all Slocum got in way of criticism of the way Kent did his job.

"I heard tell he rode along on that lawyer's coattails," Slocum said. "What's his name? Farnsworth?"

"Yeah, him. He's tryin' to buy all the best claims," Marv said. "Farnsworth's an all right guy, but he owns Kent lock, stock, and barrel. We should get paid as well as the marshal does." This brought a round of laughter. Slocum smiled but didn't join in. He had no quarrel with Kent.

The man had found out about Slocum's past and was willing to look the other way. A dead judge over in Georgia meant nothing to the people of Precious, Idaho. To Kent it might mean a reward to supplement a meager income. For this overlooking of past misdeeds, Slocum was feeling beholden to the marshal.

What else the marshal might do was matter to be decided.

"How are you gents intending to keep down the robberies?" Slocum asked. He had about given up on the whim of robbing the stage from Coeur d'Alene. With dozens of gun-toting vigilantes galloping around the countryside, he was even less inclined to make a quick buck that way.

Still, he might change his mind. The vigilante miners weren't the best guards for the mine shipments, but their presence might encourage Lucas to put a little extra into the strongbox and sweeten the robbery that much more. There wasn't a miner in the room—or any ten—that Slocum didn't feel confident in taking, if he set up an ambush just right. They'd be milling around, stepping on each other, and getting in the way when the shooting started and one or two of them got winged.

"We will, don't you worry none on that score," Marv assured him, then belched. Slocum had lost count of how many beers the vigilante had.

One of the other men reminded the group that they weren't out patrolling the streets of Precious to keep them safe for ordinary citizens. Amid some grumbling at leaving the Gold Tooth Saloon, the vigilance committee drifted out. Marv was the last to go, and Slocum watched him like a hawk. When the vigilante staggered out, Slocum finished his beer and went after him.

Marv wobbled up and down the street, three others patrolling with him. Slocum bided his time. He didn't want to rush things and make Precious too hot for him to stay. He had business with Farnsworth to settle. And he wanted to see Lurene Macmillan again, if only to tell her what had gone on out at her brother's mine.

Slocum moved like a ghost, drifting from one doorway to another. The sun was dipping behind the distant mountain peaks and bathing the town in soft gray shadows. When Marv belched, said something, and staggered away from the other vigilantes, Slocum acted.

He followed Marv toward the edge of town. The man was busy working at the buttons on his fly, getting ready to take a piss. He was so intent on getting rid of the beer he had drunk, he didn't hear Slocum come up behind him. Slocum drew his Colt Navy and brought it down in a swift arc on the back of Marv's head.

Marv toppled forward and lay still in the mud. Slocum looked around and saw that his swift attack had gone unnoticed. He stepped over the fallen man and rolled him onto his side. The wanted poster still stuck out of Marv's shirt pocket. With quick fingers, Slocum snared the wanted poster and pulled it out.

Unfolding the paper, breaking off corners of the age-brittled sheet, he held it up and peered at it closely. For several seconds he wasn't sure what he was looking at. Then he laughed.

"You stupid son of a bitch," Slocum said without malice. He tucked the wanted poster back into Marv's pocket and walked off, whistling to himself.

The wanted poster hadn't been for him. He didn't recognize the man's face on the faded sheet, and the crime was for assaulting a sheriff over in Portland. Slocum couldn't remember the last time he'd been in Portland, if ever, and he would never leave behind any lawman carrying a grudge.

"Vigilantes!" Slocum snorted. Something about getting a group of well-meaning, illiterate men together to uphold the law reduced their common sense to levels a donkey would sneer at.

He walked back onto Precious's main street and saw the town was coming alive as the sun dipped lower in the west. Men poured in from the mines to slake their thirst. But something else drew most of the town's attention. Shouts from over at the stage depot drew the town's populace like flies to shit.

"They done it again!" raged the stage agent. "They done upped and took every single ounce of gold in the shipment! Isn't anyone's gold safe in this damned town?" Lucas was fit to be tied.

Vigilantes came from all over to listen to Lucas's tale of rage and woe. Slocum stood back and let Lucas rage on. A shipment of gold and silver to Coeur d'Alene had been robbed not ten miles down the road from Precious. Lost in the shipment was more than gold. The U.S. Mail had been taken, also. Letters were gone.

"What about *your* shipments out of here?" demanded Lucas. "How many of them have been lost? We sent out twenty pounds of gold on this stage. Do any of you want to risk *your* gold being robbed next time?"

"Calm down, Mr. Lucas," urged Marshal Kent. "There's no need to—"

"No need to get all worked up? Is that what you were going to say, marshal? I want protection. I can't ship *from* Precious and there's no chance of getting shipments *into* town. We lost two damned passengers the other day!"

The arguing raged on, Kent trying to calm the stage agent and the vigilance committee getting in the way of real justice. Kent wanted to form a posse to find the men responsible. The vigilantes wanted to do the catching—and hanging—on their own.

Slocum slipped away. He had heard similar arguments in the past. Somebody was going to end up with a stretched neck, guilty or not. He didn't want to be the one the vigilantes decided on. He'd already squeaked past Marv and his wanted poster.

This was as good a time as any to find Lurene and talk with her. He went past the boardinghouse and saw the lovely blond woman at the rear. She was returning from the barn.

"Miss Macmillan!" he called. "May I have a word with you?" Slocum wasn't sure who might be watching or listening. He didn't want to give the wrong impression and have Mrs. Addington throw Lurene out for loose morals.

"John!" Lurene had no such fears. She dropped a bucket filled with grain and ran to him, her arms outstretched. Slocum cast a quick look toward the house. A single light burned in the front room. Anyone might be spying on them.

The kiss Lurene gave him rocked him back for a moment. He was torn between protecting her reputation and wanting more of what she so openly offered.

"Let's go talk," he suggested, still looking around to be sure no one saw them together.

"You worry so, John," Lurene said, giggling like a school-girl. "No one in the boardinghouse cares how I spend my time. Not even Mrs. Addington, though she is like an old mother hen."

Lurene didn't press the point. Lurene was able to decide for herself whether she wanted to be a soiled dove or a proper young lady. They went to the barn where she had given him the delightful bath the night before. Slocum could hardly believe it had been less than twenty-four hours since he had been bushwhacked and had come riding back, too dazed to know where he was going.

"What did you find out?" she asked. "Did you get the deed?"

"No, I didn't. I looked for the tin can, but it wasn't under the floorboards," Slocum said. He watched her beautiful face's radiance vanish, as if a cloud had passed across the sun's disk.

"Then there's no way to prove the mine was Charles's."

"I couldn't even find his body," Slocum admitted. He didn't tell her that might be impossible. There were too many abandoned shafts in the mountains. All Howe had to do was find one and toss her brother's body down it. Or it might even be buried under tons of rock, either inside the LuLu Belle or somewhere else. Murder often went unpunished, especially when done with great planning.

"It's hopeless," she said. "I'm sorry I involved you in this. You were so kind." She threw her arms around his neck and buried her face in his shoulder. Slocum felt hot tears turning his shoulder damp.

"I met Farnsworth and his hired gun. I think they're the ones responsible," Slocum told her.

"What? You *know* who the claim jumpers are? This is wonderful! We can prove—"

"We can't prove much of anything right now," Slocum said. "Unless I misread the signs, Farnsworth has doctored the land records. He might have the marshal in his hip pocket, and he certainly is known around town. Your brother wasn't."

"Charles was always a quiet man," she said, remembering her dead brother. "He never caused any trouble."

"If he had, we'd have a better chance of showing that Farnsworth is a claim jumper. If your brother had raised a little hell and made folks in Precious notice him more, they'd remember he had claimed the LuLu Belle."

"There are so many mines," Lurene said almost wistfully.

"That's the problem. Hundreds of them. The shop keepers don't much remember unless the miner asks for credit. And that doesn't put your brother with any particular claim. He might have been working any hole in the ground."

"But it was his," protested Lurene. "I refuse to simply let these ruffians kill him and take what he worked so hard to develop."

"I'm not saying we roll over and play dead," Slocum cut in, heading off a long jeremiad.

"So, John? What do you suggest we do? We can't get a clear title to the mine. No one in Precious knew my brother. And the law is bought and paid for by this Farnsworth."

Slocum didn't answer directly. He knew Marv the vigilante had no notion who coldcocked him. The vigilance committee might prove an interesting mix in the heady stew Slocum intended to prepare.

"We start by going to the mine. Farnsworth and Howe aren't going to camp out there. They have other fish to fry."

"Other claims to steal, you mean," Lurene said, her mouth set in a thin, angry line.

"That's right. And if they can't pay much attention to the LuLu Belle, that means you might get the mine back. Get your things. You're going to become a squatter."

Slocum went to the gunsmith just before the shop closed for the night and bought a tool for working on his Colt Navy. The precision six-shooter needed some work to keep it in perfect condition. Then he bought enough .37 caliber ammunition to stand off an army. Slocum didn't intend to get into a prolonged fight, but if it came down to shooting, he wanted to be prepared.

By the time he got enough food for them to last two weeks, Lurene Macmillan was ready. He loaded her belongings and their supplies into the back of the buckboard. Night cloaked much of the loading. If anyone spied on them, they wouldn't have a clue what was going on.

"John, I have a question," Lurene said almost shyly.

"What?" Slocum wasn't sure what she was going to ask. It was probably about their sleeping arrangements out at the mine. The cabin had only a single room. But she surprised him.

"What is a squatter? It sounds—ugly."

Slocum laughed heartily. Lurene was a never-ending source of amazement for him. She was lovely, sharp as a knife's blade, and yet she was naive in many ways.

"We go out and just move in. Then Farnsworth has to figure out how best to throw us off the property without causing too much of a ruckus. I want that to be hard for him to do."

"All he need do is get a court order. The marshal will remove us and put us in jail if we don't obey."

Slocum grinned wickedly. "That's going to cause a commotion in town. If the townspeople see you as the injured party, they might force Farnsworth's hand."

"I see. You'd tell them Farnsworth and Howe might kill them and steal *their* claims, as they did Charles's."

"Vigilance committees are strange beasts. They don't follow the law too often. More like a man getting punched. He
jerks back in response, never giving any thought to what he's
doing."

"So we want the vigilantes to side with us?"

"Why not make them useful? All they're likely to do
otherwise is chase their own tails and maybe hang some
innocent person."

"I'm not sure I'd want Farnsworth hanged," Lurene said
after considering it. "Even if he did kill Charles. It would be
better to put him in prison and try to reform him."

Slocum snorted in contempt at the notion. Nobody reasoned
with a mad dog. You either got out of its way or you shot it.
Anything else meant you got bitten. Farnsworth was more
refined, but he couldn't be controlled by gentle reason.

"One step at a time," Slocum said. "First we establish a
claim on the LuLu Belle, even if we have to start as squatters.
Then we worry about Farnsworth and how he and Howe
murdered your brother." He was harsher than he'd meant.
Lurene seemed to shrivel a little, wrapping her arms around
herself on the buckboard seat beside him. Slocum didn't care.
She was lovely, but she needed a good dose of how things
were done on the frontier.

They drove steadily for the mine, the hour-long trip lit
by the waning moon. Slocum jumped out and made sure
the sign pointing the way to the claim was in place. Then
he opened a small can of red paint he had bought at the
general store and added, Owner: Lurene Macmillan to the
bottom.

"Doesn't hurt to advertise our presence," Slocum said,
getting back into the buckboard. "Anybody passing by in
the morning will notice the fresh paint. They might wonder
who you are, or even come up to pay a neighborly visit."

"It's unusual for a woman's name to be listed as owner of a mine, isn't it?"

Slocum didn't bother telling her that miners had a healthy fear of women even being near mines. Most were superstitious and thought a woman in a shaft meant immediate danger. And the land laws in Idaho didn't allow an unmarried woman to own any real property.

These were minor points, but ones Slocum counted on to draw as much attention as possible to the LuLu Belle. Farnsworth was like a snake in the night. As long as darkness hid his actions, he was safe. The bright light of notoriety might force his hand.

"John," Lurene said, as they got within a hundred feet of the cabin, "something's wrong."

"What is it?" Slocum's hand went to his six-shooter. He had a good sense of danger and didn't feel anything close, but he wasn't taking any chances. The entire area was shadowy and a small army could be lying in ambush.

"The cabin's not where it should be. It's been moved. Is that possible?"

"Moved?" Slocum looked uphill and saw where the cabin might have been built. It was a tad closer to the mine shaft where it stood, but now that Lurene mentioned it, he saw skid marks on the rock.

"Yes, it was higher on the hill. And the mine is all closed. There was a collapse!"

"I told you about it. Somebody dynamited the opening."

"But, oh, I didn't think it would look this hopeless. There's so much debris. We'll never be able to clear it out."

"It'll look better in broad daylight. Your brother did a good job sinking his shaft into solid rock," Slocum pointed out. He could work the mine and get some of the tunnel free and even pull out some pay dirt, but he had no intention of working the claim the rest of his life. He was earning his fifty percent share and as soon as the title was free and clear, he would sell his part and move on.

Slocum looked at Lurene and wondered what she would do after they won this fight. She might end up rich or she might come away empty-handed. And would the money even matter that much to her? The moonlight turned her blond hair to flowing silver. Small shadows danced across her face as she moved and turned her into an angel come to earth. She wasn't the kind to marry a miner and live in a line shack the rest of her life. She would be happiest marrying a prosperous banker or storekeeper and raising a family in some comfortable, civilized Eastern city.

Then he remembered her passion when they'd made love in the barn behind the boardinghouse. Slocum shook his head and wondered if he would ever know women. Lurene was complex and too much for him to figure out in this lifetime.

"We'll look into that in the morning," he said, climbing down. He looked to his Appaloosa. The horse was tethered to the rear of the buckboard and had quietly trotted along behind all the way from town without any protest. Now it snorted and pulled back at the rope that tied it.

Slocum spun to see what had spooked his horse and drew his Colt. He saw the shadow figure in the cabin's doorway an instant before a long orange tongue of flame licked out at him and a bullet tore past his head.

He returned fire, not knowing who—or how many—he fought.

9

"Take cover!" Slocum shouted to Lurene. The woman sat in the buckboard as if frozen to the wood seat. Two more bullets whined through the night. One dug a splinter out of the buckboard's seat an inch from her. This startled her into motion. She dived out as if she had burst into flame.

Slocum fired twice more and drove the man in the cabin's doorway back inside. He took the opportunity to grab the Winchester sheathed on his saddle. Levering a round into the chamber, he was ready for serious gunplay.

Slocum saw that Lurene had taken cover behind a pile of rocks thrown from the mine by the dynamiting that had almost cost him his life. She was as safe as possible until he got rid of the man ambushing them. Slocum let off a round that tore through the cabin's thin wall. The bullet didn't ricochet around inside as he'd hoped, but he knew it would keep the unseen gunman honest, or at least make him think twice about poking his head out again.

Circling the cabin, Slocum came up to it from the mountainside. He doubted the man inside was going to bolt and run, but if he did, Slocum wanted to be in position to get a good shot. He scrambled up a pile of loose shale, then jumped, catching the edge of the roof and pulling himself up.

The roof sagged under his weight. It would never have survived an Idaho winter's load of snow. But maybe Charles Macmillan hadn't intended to stay that long. Winter this far north drove more than a few men farther south until the spring thaws. Slocum slipped on the slick roof and was rewarded with a bullet blasting upward not a foot from his body. He paused, trying not to move, not wanting to give any clues to the man in the cabin.

"John, are you all right?" Lurene shouted.

Slocum cursed under his breath. If he answered, he might get drilled by the man beneath him. If he didn't answer, Lurene might come to see if he had been injured.

Rolling fast, hoping to avoid new bullets, Slocum moved to the hole cut in the roof for the stove vent. The stovepipe was missing and, if Slocum remembered rightly, so was the stove. He poked his rifle through the hole and began firing wildly. He didn't care if he hit his ambusher as much as he wanted to keep him hopping.

The tactic must have worked, because no return fire came. Slocum didn't believe for an instant that he'd killed the man in the cabin. He doubted he had even winged him. Both of them had to play cagey or there would be a new grave nearby.

Slocum vowed it wasn't going to be his.

"John, are you hurt? Answer me!"

Slocum continued to ignore Lurene, then knew he couldn't when she rose and started tentatively moving toward the cabin. He dropped his empty rifle and drew his Colt Navy. He tried to remember how many rounds he had fired and couldn't. He had at least three shots left, but probably not four. He just couldn't remember.

Slocum made his way to the front of the cabin and peered over the edge of the roof, waiting for the man inside to target

Lurene. To his surprise, the door didn't budge. And there weren't any windows to fire through.

"John?"

"Get down!" Slocum shouted. He dropped flat on his belly and thrust his six-shooter over the edge of the roof, waiting to fire when the man inside made a move. He didn't find a target.

"I see someone over there," Lurene called, pointing behind Slocum. He glanced over his shoulder in time to see a shadow flitting into a stand of trees too small to be any good for timbers to shore up a mine. Charles Macmillan probably intended to cut them down and burn them as firewood later.

Slocum swung and fired twice, knowing he couldn't hit anyone at this range except by pure chance. Lady Luck didn't ride with him in his shots. He dropped from the roof and crouched down until he advanced to kick open the door. He spun into the cabin, ready to use his last round.

Empty.

He made a quick circuit and found two floorboards yanked up. Their ambusher had sneaked out while Slocum was on the roof firing into the empty cabin. His luck was turning from bad to worse. All he had done was waste ammo.

"John, don't go after him. Stay here with me," urged Lurene.

Slocum began reloading his six-shooter. He wasn't going to let any back shooter get away without a fight. Ignoring Lurene's protests, he set off to bag him a killer. He didn't know if this was the same man who had tried back shooting him on the road or had killed Kenny Moore or if it was someone entirely different. For all he knew, Precious was filled to the brim with murderous swine intent on ventilating him from behind.

But this one wasn't going to get away.

Slocum stalked the man, wary that he wasn't being led into a trap. He struggled to hear any sounds of the man's escape. Nothing but the soft sighing of wind through lodgepole pines higher on the mountain came to him. Slocum hunkered down, pistol thrust out in front of him. He waited for several minutes.

He didn't hear anything, so he began working his way deeper into the stand of head-high trees. When he came to the far side, the mountain stretched above and below, and he had lost the fugitive's trail entirely. Slocum studied the ground for any spoor. Try as he might, he didn't see so much as a scuffed rock or broken twig. Their ambusher might have just vanished into thin air.

To be sure he wasn't wrong, Slocum settled down and waited for another ten minutes. His every sense strained to hear the man he sought. Nothing. Cursing, Slocum returned to Charles Macmillan's cabin. Lurene was beside herself with worry.

"John, you're all right!"

She threw her arms around his neck and clung to him. She sobbed softly and then managed to control herself. Blue eyes looked up at him, silvered from moonlight reflecting off her tears.

"I've lost my mother and father. I've lost Charles. I don't want to lose you, too." She buried her face once more in his chest. It took her almost a minute to compose herself enough to push back. She straightened her skirts and looked resolute.

"It's time to get settled down for the evening," she said. "We've had enough excitement for a while."

"Are you worried about him coming back?" Slocum asked.

Lurene paused a moment, then a grin crossed her face. She shook her head and sent blond curls rippling. "Not with you here. You ran him off good and proper. Nobody but a fool would come back to tangle with you and that six-gun of yours."

She pressed her fingertips into his chest, then worked them down lower to rest on his rock-hard belly. Lurene looked up again, then tipped her head back slightly. Her eyes closed and her lips pursed.

Slocum kissed her. She threw her arms around his neck and pulled him down even harder. Their kiss deepened with passion, and Slocum felt himself responding. He knew he ought to stand guard. He hadn't run that trespasser off for good. Danger might return at any instant.

And Slocum didn't give a damn.

All he knew was the warm, willing woman in his arms. He swept her up and carried her into the cabin. The floor was uneven, but it wasn't dirt. He laid Lurene down gently, then began unfastening his gun belt. He laid his Colt Navy to one side where he could reach it if the need arose. Somehow, he doubted that it would. Looking down at Lurene told him everything was going to be just fine for the rest of the night.

"I want you, John," the blond said softly. A single ray of moonlight came through the stovepipe hole in the roof and bathed her face. He reached out and touched her cheek, then ran his hand down the side of her throat. His strong fingers lingered for a moment to unfasten the buttons on her dress. She scooted around a little and was naked to the waist.

Slocum's fingers reached under her, cupped her firm buttocks, and lifted. Lurene silently followed his movement. He stripped off her dress and cast it aside. He caught his breath as he looked at her naked beauty. Never had he seen such a gorgeous woman. She was slender, trim, and even better, she wanted him as badly as he did her.

Lurene sat up, her breasts bouncing slightly. He caught the coppery nipples and fondled them. She sighed and shoved her chest forward so that the flesh crushed hard into his hands. He squeezed and she let out a tiny sigh of joy.

Then she began working on his clothes. She'd pull open a button, then kiss the exposed flesh. He felt her hot breath gusting down the front of his chest. As she worked lower, the heat from her mouth excited him more and more. By the time she skinned him out of his jeans, he was hard and ready for her.

"Now, John. Don't wait. I need you now."

"And I need you," he said, moving to the space formed by the vee of her legs. He dropped down and she reached to catch his rigid shaft. He groaned as she crushed down hard on his length. Then she tugged insistently, getting him forward.

Slocum felt the softness of her nether lips, then worked his way forward another inch. Lurene gasped with the insertion. Slocum held himself on stiffened arms for a moment, savoring the warmth surrounding his tip.

Then he began arching his back even more, sending himself deeper into her yearning interior. When he was buried balls deep, he paused and relished the feel of gripping female flesh all around him. Slocum moved his hips in a small circle, as if he were using a spoon to stir in a mixing bowl.

The motion drove Lurene wild with need. She arched her back and rammed her hips down hard around him.

"Do it, John, do it now. I can't wait. I'm burning up inside."

He began withdrawing slowly, tormenting her, getting the most thrill he could from the movement. When he was almost out, he drove back into her—hard.

She let out a gasp of pure ecstasy. Her fingers clawed at his back and her legs circled his waist. Lurene locked her heels behind him to be sure he wouldn't run off. Slocum had no intention of leaving her now. His loins burned with desire for her and he was surrendering totally to his emotions.

He thrust back and paused once more. He bent over and toyed with her nipples, using only the tip of his tongue. This drove her wild with lust. Lurene began bucking and thrashing under him until Slocum felt the tightness of her squeeze down even more. He thought he was trapped in a warm, velvet tunnel and was being crushed.

Slocum pulled back against the power of the woman's legs wrapped around his hips. He used that tension to drive back in. He fell into the age-old rhythm of a man loving a woman.

Lurene started making small trapped-animal noises, but Slocum couldn't stop. Not now. He felt the blond woman stiffen and then cry out under him. He kept moving, stroking, burning them both up with the friction of his touch.

"John, yes, no, don't stop. Oh, I love you, John, I love you!"

Slocum exploded within her. Spent, he sank down to lay atop Lurene Macmillan. Then he rolled to one side. He was covered with sweat and felt a curious mixture of exhaustion and elation.

"Damn, but you are about the prettiest woman I've ever seen," he said.

"Everything will work out just fine, John," she said, curling up next to him. Lurene rested her head on his shoulder. Within minutes, she was asleep.

Slocum lay with his arm around Lurene's naked shoulders and stared at the cabin's roof. Holes had been poked through from his rolling around up there. Here and there Slocum saw stars in the clear Idaho sky. Stars. Freedom to wander under them. He'd never be able to do that if he stayed with Lurene.

But he'd be a doubly damned fool if he passed on a woman this loving and lovely.

Sleep finally took him, but he awoke with a start in just a few hours. Sunlight poured through the cabin door and he heard the horses outside protesting the lack of food and water.

Slocum pulled his arm from under Lurene's head and eased her to the floor. He gathered her dress and bundled it up for her to use as a pillow now that he was gone. She didn't seem to mind being naked on the rough floor. Slocum rubbed his own hindquarters. He had picked up a splinter or two sleeping without a bedroll, but he didn't mind that much when he remembered how they had come to be on the floor.

Dressing quickly, Slocum strapped on his six-shooter and went outside. His Appaloosa was pawing the ground impatiently, and the swayback mare hitched to the buckboard looked at him eagerly, hoping he would feed her.

Slocum staked the two horses near a patch of new grass and then worked at the well to pull up enough water for the animals. He poured a bucket over his own head and then went back to drawing water. This was going to be a long day.

He had hardly begun pawing through the rubble at the mine's mouth when he heard Lurene up and moving around. She joined him after a few minutes, looking better than any woman had a right to.

"I worried when I woke and you were gone," she said. "Then I saw you tending the horses."

"Everything's going just fine," he told her. He felt suddenly shy, in spite of what they'd done last night. Feeling like a schoolboy, he bent and gave her a quick kiss. Lurene beamed.

"I'd better fix us some breakfast. What would you like?"

"No druthers in the matter," Slocum told her. He wondered how good a cook she was. In less than twenty minutes, he found out. She had prepared a meal tastier than anything he had ever fixed for himself on the trail. He got mighty tired of beans and salt pork. Lurene had fixed bacon and two of the eggs he had bought in town. With them she rustled up biscuits and had even found some jam in the supplies he hadn't known was there.

As he ate, he studied the mine. Opening it again would be a month's work. The dynamiter had done his job well, almost too well for Slocum's taste.

"I can get the best of the ore moved down the mountainside," he told Lurene. "We might be able to use some of that medium-grade ore to pay for what's to come."

"Farnsworth?"

"Sooner or later, he'll be out here. He'll bluster and threaten, but I don't think he'll loose Howe. Getting the marshal to evict us will be easier and more legal. When that doesn't work, we'll be in for a real fight."

"We watch our backs every second," she said grimly. "I wish Charles had known what he was up against."

"Farnsworth might have considered him to be a rock-headed miner without any good sense. Killing him was easier and cheaper than buying the LuLu Belle." Slocum sopped up the last of the bacon grease on his tin plate with a biscuit. The last bite was a good as the first. Lurene was a good cook.

"We've got to make it up so expensive for him to get us out that he'll give up—or make a big mistake." Slocum wiped off his plate and stuck it back into their supply cache.

Lurene looked around, frowning. "Where do you think they left Charles's body?" she asked.

"Don't go searching for it," Slocum cautioned. "Stay close to camp for the time being. We'll tackle one problem at a time."

His sharp eyes saw the cloud of dust rising from the direction of the main road. For a moment, the dust vanished, then kicked up in a tall column. Someone had seen the freshly painted sign and was coming up to the mine in a hurry.

Slocum didn't have to be a mind reader to know who it was.

"What the hell's going on?" shouted Farnsworth. Behind him Stanton Howe rested his hand on his six-shooter.

"We decided to keep working Miss Macmillan's claim, even though her brother's taken off for a spell." Slocum wanted Farnsworth to admit to killing Charles Macmillan, but the lawyer was too cunning to make such an admission.

"This is my property. Get off it right now."

"Reckon we'll stay. Miss Macmillan's brother owns this claim. You can't prove any different." Slocum widened his stance and moved his jacket away from the ebony butt of his Colt Navy. He could blow Howe out of the saddle before the gunman drew his six-gun. Howe wore his hogleg hanging at his right hip with the butt poking backward, making it awkward for him to draw while he was on horseback.

"Where is her brother?" demanded Farnsworth. "I own this claim, not anyone else. I'll have it out with him."

"We're here. He isn't," Slocum said.

"Let me run them off, boss," spoke up Howe. The man went for his gun as he spoke, thinking to gull Slocum into a moment's hesitation.

Slocum's pistol cleared leather before Howe could throw down on him. Slocum's slug tore through the brim of Howe's hat and sent it sailing through the air. The gunman was so startled he jerked around and fell from his horse.

"If he goes for his gun again, he's a dead man, and so are you," Slocum said. The ice-and-steel edge to his voice convinced Howe to open his hand and get them away from his six-shooter.

"We'll be back," Farnsworth snarled. "We'll get a court order and have you arrested for claim jumping. You wait and see."

"Say howdy to Marshal Kent for me," Slocum called as Farnsworth turned and rode off angrily. Howe followed, looking over his shoulder. He looked daggers at Slocum.

When those two rode back, the meeting wouldn't be so pleasant.

10

"There's going to be real trouble now, isn't there?" Lurene Macmillan asked. She stood behind Slocum, her hand on his shoulder. She was shaking so hard he had to turn and take her hand away.

"You knew what we were facing when we came out to squat on this claim. If Farnsworth sticks with legal action, we've got him beat seven ways to Sunday. It's when he switches to bushwhacking, then we've got to be ready for him."

"John," Lurene said, a tremor in her voice. "I didn't know this would turn so ugly."

Slocum laughed harshly. It hadn't turned ugly yet. And three times someone had tried to dry-gulch him. It would be an all-out war when the shooting started.

"Don't mock me," she said, tears forming in her eyes. She dabbed at one as it started to leak out.

"You've lost your family," Slocum said. "I'm not making fun of you. Do you want to give up now?"

"No!" she shot back. "I owe Charles this much. But this isn't your fight. You didn't know what you were getting involved in when you agreed to help me. I'm saying that I won't hold you to our agreement."

"You're trying to welsh on giving me half the mine?" Slocum asked.

"No, not that. I just thought you might want to just ride on." Her blue eyes overflowed with tears now. She didn't bother trying to stop them or dam up the flow.

Slocum didn't answer directly. He knew how he must look to her. He was a drifter without roots or convictions. That might be how he looked to others, but deep down inside, Slocum was different. He had seen too much suffering in his day, and it had hardened him. It had also made him unwilling to let men like Farnsworth and Howe run roughshod over those who couldn't protect themselves.

"You don't know me too well," he said slowly. "I never go back on my promises. And if you quit, that won't much matter to me."

This startled Lurene. She looked at him hard and asked, "Why not? Aren't you doing this for me, because I asked, because of Charles?"

"I'm doing this for myself," Slocum said. Nobody could try to kill Slocum and get away with it. It never paid to leave someone trying to kill you behind your back. He needed to be sure Farnsworth and Howe were the ones responsible for trying to dynamite him and backshoot him, but facts just didn't fit. Kenny Moore getting shot in the back was just a part of it.

And who had been in the cabin when he and Lurene had ridden up? From Farnsworth's reaction, it hadn't been him or his gunman. They seemed genuinely surprised and angered that Slocum and Lurene had moved in on the LuLu Belle. If either of them had been nosing around the night before, there was no need for them to pretend to be outraged. More to the issue, Farnsworth would have returned with a small army— or Marshal Kent and a restraining order.

"You'll stay?" she asked in a quavering voice. "Really?"

"I'm doing this for my own reasons. If you stay on and fight and get clear title to the mine, I surely wouldn't turn down half ownership. But that's not important any longer."

"Thank you," Lurene said. She hugged Slocum hard, then kissed him quickly. Slocum didn't know what to say but didn't have to worry on it. Lurene backed off, wiped her tears, and then rushed off to the cabin. Slocum watched her go and tried to sort out what he felt for her.

He had meant every word he said about continuing the fight, even if she quit. But Slocum realized now he had been counting on Lurene to back down. She hadn't, and he didn't know what to do next.

He looked at the tumble of rock in the mouth of the LuLu Belle, then looked over the side of the mountain to where the cabin might have stood before sliding down. Somewhere in the softer dirt up there might be a baking soda can with Charles Macmillan's claim to the mine in it. Slocum considered how much work it would take to find this needle in a haystack and decided his time could be better spent in Precious.

He went to the cabin and poked his head inside. Lurene was doing what she could to turn the bare shed into livable quarters. The blond looked up and asked, "What is it, John?"

"I don't think there will be any trouble here for a few hours. I'm going into Precious and stir up the town against Farnsworth."

Lurene laughed, and it sounded genuine. "That might not take much doing. I never heard anyone say much good about him."

"He's from Coeur d'Alene. That makes him as much an outsider as we are," Slocum said. A mining community was made up of a lot of footloose men and a few loose women, but they quickly welded together. Fire, mining disasters, and the common bond of getting drunk together all made them a community. The quickness with which the vigilance committee had formed only showed how much the people of Precious thought of their town and its safety.

"I'll be fine. I have a rifle and know how to use it." Lurene indicated an old Henry rifle leaning against the wall. Slocum doubted she knew how to hit anything with it, but if she could load and fire it, that might be good enough.

"I won't be too long. I'll be back by midafternoon." He looked back down the mountainside and knew that Lurene was safe here for the time being. "Why don't you go uphill a ways and see if you can sift through the dirt and find your brother's deed."

"Of course!" she cried. "That hadn't occurred to me before. If the cabin was higher up, the baking soda tin would be there!"

Slocum gave Lurene a quick kiss, lingered a mite, then forced himself to saddle his Appaloosa and ride back toward Precious. The woman was a powerful attraction for him, but he had work to do. And it wasn't honest work, the way Slocum saw it.

He tried to figure what Farnsworth would do. Getting a court order to evict Lurene from the mine would take too long. Farnsworth would have to ride to Coeur d'Alene or find a circuit judge to get the legal process started. Not only would it take too long, Farnsworth would feel his authority was being challenged. He didn't dare let a woman stay on the claim or his strong-arm techniques might begin to fail with other miners.

Slocum decided Farnsworth would convince Marshal Kent that he had to go arrest the claim jumpers. The marshal was undoubtedly in the lawyer's pay, but public pressure could sway Kent. Slocum didn't think the marshal would stand long against the power of Precious's fledgling vigilance committee.

He dismounted in front of the Gold Tooth Saloon. A half dozen horses were tethered out front and drinking from the saloon's trough. The horses' owners were inside, bellied up to the bar. Slocum touched his pocket and felt the wad of greenbacks there. He had about half his poker winnings left. He reckoned it was time to spend some of it to grease the way—and the vigilantes' gullets.

"Howdy," he called, pushing into the center of the men. They were all armed and had the look of men who had been on a long, hot, dusty patrol—an unsuccessful one. "What you gents been up to? Catching crooks?"

"Don't we wish," said one man. He wearily rolled the ends of his mustache. "We been chasin' down shadows. I swear those road agents are too danged clever by half."

"Aw, Phil, we'll get 'em. Just give us time. We only started," said another.

"That's right," chimed in Slocum. "You're only just learning their ways. And did any stagecoach get robbed today?"

"No, can't say one did," said Phil. "Why do you ask?"

"Just goes to show how successful you were," Slocum said. "You kept those varmints from holding up any stage today." He didn't bother asking if one had even been scheduled that day.

"Yeah, right. Never thought of it that way. I guess we were doin' better 'n any of us thought," said Phil.

"Let me buy you gents a drink for your good work," Slocum said. The barkeep beamed and set up a round of freshly brewed beers for the vigilantes. Slocum drank slowly, letting them get to know him.

Finally, he said, "I've been fighting a battle of my own, you know." Slocum waited for a response. When it came, he continued, "That lawyer fellow from over in Coeur d'Alene. You know him. Farnsworth."

"Oh, that slimy son of a buck," said Phil. "Yeah, we all know him. Him and his hired gun are always sniffing around our claims."

"That's what he's doing out at the LuLu Belle. He's making wild demands on how Miss Lurene Macmillan ought to get away from her brother's claim while her brother's back East with his family." Slocum let the lie flow easily. The men wouldn't believe him if he said Charles Macmillan was dead, and even if they did, there was no way he could indict Farnsworth for the crime. This way was better. And if any of them knew Macmillan was dead, that pointed a finger at him as being a murderer.

"Well, Slocum, don't you worry none about him. We've been keepin' the road agents at bay from the stage. We can make certain Farnsworth don't bother you and the little lady none till her brother gets back."

Slocum shrugged and finished his beer. "That's real neighborly of you, but it might not be Farnsworth who comes a-calling." He let the men sort out what he really meant. It didn't take long. Phil was quick on the uptake.

"You mean he'll send his toady Kent out? Shucks, Slocum, that's no more of a worry than Farnsworth ought to be. We can handle the marshal, can't we, boys?"

The cheer that went up deafened Slocum. He approved of their enthusiasm, even if he hated the notion of a vigilance committee taking the law into its own hands. He didn't often agree with the law, but leaving it to the local sheriff or marshal was a damned sight better than having a dozen men driven by liquor and blood lust on the loose.

"Are they givin' you trouble right now, Slocum?" asked Phil.

"Might be," Slocum said. "I came into town to talk with the marshal, but I haven't been able to find him." Slocum didn't add that he had come straight into the Gold Tooth when he saw the crowd of vigilantes.

"Well, men, let's go help ol' Slocum out then. And the little lady. We don't want the womenfolk gettin' tromped on by any Coeur d'Alene lawyer!" This was met with a cheer. Slocum allowed himself to be carried along with the crowd. He hadn't intended going straight back to the mine, but it appeared to be a good idea.

The only problem he saw was the lack of liquor out at the LuLu Belle to keep the vigilantes content until Farnsworth and his hired men showed up.

The hour's ride back was a boisterous one. Slocum had formed his plans carefully while riding into Precious. Going back to the mine required all his tact to keep the men from getting into fights among themselves and arguing over how best to rid the territory of what they saw as the lawless element.

Lurene was startled to see Slocum riding up with a small army. She put down the old rifle and wiped sweat from her forehead. She had been working and was grimy from the dirt, but Slocum still had never seen a prettier woman. There didn't seem to be anything Lurene could do to look dowdy.

"We'll just set up a patrol to keep this here place safe," Phil said. He had come forth as the leader on the ride out. Slocum wasn't sure who Phil was, but he looked like some down on his luck miner. The vigilance committee might consist more of failed miners than of men worried about crime in their midst.

"John," Lurene said when the vigilantes spread out, "what are we going to do with them if Farnsworth doesn't come out?"

"Don't rightly know," Slocum said, smiling slightly. He didn't much care if a pitched battle occurred because the vigilantes would go back to Precious and brag about how they had defended a claim against predatory lawyers. The talk would be as good—maybe better—than actually facing down Farnsworth.

Slocum and Lurene went up the hill and began sifting through the dirt, looking for her brother's deed. Slocum tried to figure out why the cabin had slid. The best he could tell, someone had moved it by putting a long tree limb over a rock and getting the house off its base and rumbling down the mountain. But why?

He frowned as he considered this. He was missing something, and he didn't know what. There was something about the cabin that wasn't right. His thoughts were interrupted when Lurene shook his arm and pointed down the road.

A cloud of dust rose. Three or four riders were approaching.

"We've got company," he said loud enough to alert any of the vigilantes who might be listening. He didn't get an immediate response, but that was all right. Slocum wanted personally to see who Farnsworth had rousted from the comfort of the town to come out.

"What do we do?" asked Lurene, wringing her hands. Slocum saw that for all her resolution to keep fighting to bring her brother's murderers to justice, she was having a hard time facing the men.

Slocum went down the hill, wiped the dirt from his hands, and made sure the leather thong was free of his Colt's hammer. He was ready for whatever happened. A slow smile crossed his face when he saw Farnsworth, Howe, and Marshal Kent riding up.

"There they are, Marshal. Do your job. Get them the hell off my property!"

"I'll handle this, Mr. Farnsworth," Kent said, dismounting. He pushed back his hat and came over to stand in front of

Slocum. The marshal looked him up and down, then shook his head. "Slocum, what do you think you're doing out here?"

"I know what I'm doing, Marshal," Slocum said. "I'm protecting Miss Macmillan's claim."

"Women can't own mines. You know that."

"She's just staying here until her brother gets back. Charles Macmillan owns the LuLu Belle Mine. I don't know where Farnsworth gets the idea he has any right to be here."

Kent looked over his shoulder and motioned Farnsworth to silence. He heaved a deep sigh, then said, "I got to run you off, Slocum. This is Mr. Farnsworth's property. He's got all the legal papers to prove it. You don't have squat."

"He might have the papers, but that doesn't make the mine his. The LuLu Belle belongs to Charles Macmillan."

"Where is this Charles Macmillan?" shouted Farnsworth. "He doesn't exist. Who's ever seen him?"

"I reckon I have," came a voice from Slocum's left. Phil wandered over, fingering his rifle as he came to a halt beside Slocum. "It took a while, but I remember helping him load supplies to come out here."

"What's going on, Kent? Get them *all* off my property." Farnsworth was livid. Slocum saw Howe turn slightly to be able to pull his six-shooter and start shooting. The gunman froze when other vigilantes began making their way from their hiding places.

"What is going on, Slocum?" asked the marshal.

"These men are worried Farnsworth might do to them what he's trying to do to Miss Macmillan's brother."

"Enough of this. Where is her brother? Get him out here, and we'll talk it over with him."

"He's gone back East. We're taking care of his mine for him until he gets back."

Kent looked at the dynamited mouth of the tunnel and shook his head. "I can't force you off the land until Mr. Farnsworth gets the court orders, but he will. You know it. Make it easy on yourself."

Slocum didn't answer. Farnsworth sputtered incoherently and Kent mounted his horse and started back toward Precious without a word to the lawyer. Farnsworth urged his horse forward and glowered at Slocum.

"Mark my words, you're a dead man. Dead! Get off my property if you and the bitch want to keep breathing Idaho air!"

Slocum watched as Farnsworth and Howe rode off. The vigilantes cheered. They thought they had backed the marshal and the lawyer down. Slocum knew that wasn't what had happened. They whooped and hollered and pounded each other on the back. Slocum waited for what he knew would come next—and it did.

"We're going on back to town to celebrate, Slocum. You and the little lady want to come with us?"

"Thanks for the help, Phil. You go on back. We'll join you later, after we finish some chores here."

The vigilantes rode off, still congratulating themselves. Lurene watched them with wide eyes. "Don't they understand this doesn't mean a thing?" she asked Slocum.

"They don't understand what they're doing," Slocum said. "And they sure as hell don't realize how much power they've got in their hands right now." He looked around. It was getting toward twilight, the sun dipping down. He didn't know how much time he had before danger walked into the LuLu Belle camp, but it wouldn't be long.

"Get your rifle and go over to that stand of trees," Slocum said, pointing to where the mysterious figure had vanished the night before. "If anyone comes through there, shoot them."

"What are you going to do, John?" She looked frightened. Slocum hoped she wouldn't open up on him by mistake.

"Wait," he said simply. "Just wait."

Slocum took his Winchester and settled down some distance from the cabin. He wasn't sure how long it would take Howe to get back, but he didn't think it would be long. Slocum dozed a little, wishing he had stayed with Lurene. She might be panicking by now, jumping at every bird squawk and animal scamper. But he was so tired.

Slocum came awake when he heard the roar of the fire. He swung around, his rifle seeking a target. The cabin was on fire. And from inside he heard Lurene's screams.

11

"Lurene!" Slocum shouted, his mouth going dry with dread. He started toward the burning cabin, then he pulled back. Either Farnsworth or Howe had started the fire, and he didn't know where they were. Slocum heard Lurene scream again. The woman was trapped inside the burning cabin.

He couldn't wait to find Howe.

Slocum sprinted for the cabin. A bullet cut through the night and sent his broad-brimmed hat flying. Slocum grabbed his injured forehead. The hat, as it flew off, had ripped open his wound again. Slocum fired wildly as he ran, not knowing where Howe was hidden but wanting to keep the man down. Somehow, Slocum didn't think Farnsworth would do his own dirty work. The lawyer would be someplace visible so no one could possibly blame him for any devilment done.

"John, I can't get out!" Lurene shouted. "Help me. Help!" The shrillness in her voice told Slocum how close to outright panic she was. He admired her courage to this point, but if she let hysteria seize her, she was dead.

Another bullet sang close to Slocum, but he dodged away from it and got to the cabin door. Heat billowed out and scorched his eyebrows. Slocum got his bandanna up to cover his nose and mouth. Smoke caused tears to sting his eyes. He didn't bother calling out for Lurene. The crackle and pop of the fire would have drowned out his message.

Ducking down, Slocum bulled into the cabin. Flames licked at his arms and legs and threatened to set his hair on fire. He blinked hard and let tears wash out the greasy smoke. Through the heat and flowing tears, he saw Lurene huddled down at the far side of the cabin. Distant gunfire sounded; it took him a few seconds to realize it was Lurene's rifle going off repeatedly. The cartridges had become so hot they fired on their own.

He hoped the wild bullets wouldn't stop him as he plunged forward. His shirt began to smolder. Slocum grabbed Lurene and tried to pull her to her feet. He saw that she had passed out from too much smoke.

Keeping low, Slocum tried pulling her toward the door. The roof dropped a cascade of sparks, blocking his way. Slocum looked around, desperation growing. He lowered his shoulder and charged, hitting the wall with all his strength. The shock went through him, but the weakened wall gave way. Slocum tumbled into the night.

"Lurene, help me," he choked out. "Help yourself!" He grabbed the woman's wrists and began pulling. She coughed weakly but gave no sign of regaining consciousness. Slocum pulled harder, and the woman spilled out behind him.

Slocum rolled in the dirt and smothered the sparks threatening his shirt and pants. Then he turned to Lurene and got her clothing put out.

"Lurene, wake up. We can't stay here," he said. He shook her. The blond moaned and her blue eyes opened. She stared at him but didn't really focus.

"Why'd you go into the cabin?" he asked.

"Wanted to get—" Her voice trailed off, then she choked hard. Slocum saw she was going to be all right. What worried him was Howe or whoever had set fire to the cabin. He was still out there.

Slocum had lost his rifle in the fire, but his six-shooter was still at his hip. He lowered Lurene to the ground and went hunting for the coward who'd set fire to a cabin with a woman in it. Cautiously advancing, Slocum circled the cabin and tried to see where Howe might have gone. He dropped to one knee and looked at the softer dirt beside the cabin. Boot prints went off to the thicket where Lurene was supposed to have been standing guard. Slocum cursed. She might have winged the son of a bitch if she'd stayed at her post rather than returning to the cabin. She had given the arsonist a great opportunity for murder, and he had taken it.

Walking bent over to reduce his silhouette, Slocum got to the stand of trees and looked for spoor. He saw occasional boot prints in the dirt. Then the ground turned rockier, and he lost the trail. Slocum hurried after the fleeing owlhoot. Howe must have set the fire, taken a potshot or two at Slocum, and figured the job was done. There wasn't any other reason for him to hightail it this fast if he thought he still had some killing to do.

Slocum stopped and looked around. He had gone halfway around the mountain and had come out near Enoch Carson's Phantom Mine. The stillness of the night assured Slocum that no one was running ahead of him. He heard no horses, and most of all, he heard nothing human.

In the distance a wildcat growled. He thought riders were approaching, but after listening hard he realized it was only wind whipping through the lodgepole pines. He was alone.

And Howe—or whoever had set the fire—had gotten clean away.

Slocum paused before returning to see how Lurene was getting on. The utter silence, save for the occasional wild animal's howl, got to him. He went down the mountainside to Carson's fancy cabin and listened hard. He sniffed; no fire in the stove. In either stove, he corrected himself. The man was rich and had two stoves.

Slocum rapped on the door and got no response. He lifted the latch, then pushed the door open with his foot. Carson wasn't anywhere to be seen.

Going back outside, Slocum looked up to the mouth of the Phantom Mine. It didn't look as if Carson was working his claim, either. Slocum pushed this aside. The man was probably in town finding suckers to fleece in a poker game.

On impulse, Slocum hiked up the steep slope to the mouth of the Phantom Mine. He looked back down into the valley. No light betrayed human presence. He heard a coyote moaning in the distance. It seemed as if a mountain lion's roar was the lovelorn coyote's only answer tonight. But no people stirred.

Ducking into the mine and walking bent almost double, Slocum went a few yards until it became pitch black. He fumbled out a lucifer and lit it, holding it over his head. The back of the mine was only a few inches above him. He would never be able to stand upright in the Phantom. Slocum saw a candle and holder nearby, about where he'd expected to find them. He hastily lit the candle.

Going deeper into the mine, he saw some evidence of recent work, but not much. Not enough for Carson to buy the fancy furniture and belongings he had in his cabin.

"Maybe he spends more time playing poker than I thought," Slocum said. The miner was like a vulture swooping down on the dying miners. Carson waited for them to get drunk enough, then took whatever he could off the men. It wasn't how Slocum preferred to live, but it beat the hell out scrabbling away at poor rock like he saw along the Phantom Mine's ribs.

An occasional stope showed where Carson had tried to work a vein, but the ore wasn't high grade. Slocum remembered what the boy at the assay office had said. Some that Carson brought in was about the best in the area while other hunks of rock were well nigh worthless.

Slocum made his way out of the mine and was glad to have the high, black dome studded with stars above him again. The Phantom Mine was too tight a fit for his liking.

He hurried back to the LuLu Belle Mine and found Lurene sitting up. She just sat and stared. There weren't tears or hysterics or even outrage. She just sat and stared.

"It's all gone," she said dully. "The cabin's gone. My brother's cabin is burned to the ground."

"It wasn't much of a cabin," Slocum said, trying to comfort her. Lurene just stared. He wondered if the close call had damaged her brain. Men in battle went into shock and just stared for hours or days before cutting loose and killing anyone near them, friend or foe.

"It was about all I had of him. That and the mine. And that's all caved in." Lurene spoke in a low monotone that was scarier than if she had ranted and raved and shrieked curses.

"I couldn't find who did it, but it has to be Howe. Farnsworth sent him out to get rid of us. Why'd you go into the cabin when I told you to stay in the woods?"

"I was getting hungry and thought I would fix some food. I was searching for a can of peaches when I heard something hit the roof. Then the entire cabin seemed to explode in flame."

"He must have tossed a torch from up there," Slocum said, picking out the best spot to set the cabin afire. That jibed well with the bullets that had torn past him when he had rushed to get to the cabin. He had been prepared for Farnsworth's attack, but he hadn't thought to check Lurene and be certain she had stayed at her post.

Slocum had to keep telling himself she was an Eastern lady and not used to such things. He snorted in disgust. He wasn't used to so many attempts on his life. It was time for him to start pushing rather than waiting to be shoved.

"They won't come back. They think they got you." He thought on this and wondered if Howe might not believe he had killed both of them. "I have to go into town for a few hours."

Lurene just sat and stared.

"You will be all right, won't you?" he asked. Slocum put his finger under her chin and moved her face around so he could look her square in the eye. Only then did Lurene blink and begin to react. Shudders racked her body, but no tears came.

She threw her arms around Slocum and hugged him, then backed off a mite. "Go on, John. I can take care of myself."

Slocum wasn't so sure, but he wanted to get rid of Farnsworth and Howe right away. They wouldn't expect retaliation this quickly. He might not have to outright gun them down, he knew. It might be enough to force Farnsworth back to his offices in Coeur d'Alene.

That still didn't answer the question of bringing Charles Macmillan's killer to justice, but Slocum would take it a little at a time. He saddled his Appaloosa and rode hard back to Precious, making good time. He arrived before nine o'clock, to find the town in an uproar. He considered stopping in at the Gold Tooth Saloon for a drink, then saw that the crowd was clustered around the stage depot.

The agent, Lucas, ranted and raved and shouted for justice to be done.

Slocum dismounted and walked to the edge of the crowd to hear what was going on. It seemed that everyone in Precious had gathered to see what the commotion was about.

"I tell you, Marshal Kent's not doing anything. We need teeth for a vigilance committee!"

Such a statement from Lucas didn't surprise Slocum unduly. He remembered how incensed the agent had been at the attempted robbery a couple days earlier.

"What happened?" Slocum asked a man next to him. The miner shook his shaggy head, spat, and didn't even look in Slocum's direction.

"Terrible thing," the miner said. "The stagecoach."

"What about it? Was it robbed again?" Slocum didn't see that this would bring down the entire town. Precious was used to such robberies, and even on a slow night it wouldn't draw a crowd of this size.

"Robbed," the miner said, nodding slowly. "And the road agents done upped and killed everybody on board. The driver, the guard, four passengers. It was a bloody mess, from what I heard tell."

"We have to take the law into our own hands," came a voice Slocum recognized. Phil the vigilante climbed up next to Lucas. He seemed to be in his element now.

"We found the stage—too late. We got to protect the others since Kent ain't doin' it. The cavalry over at Fort Prosser ain't gonna give any protection. They been asked and they said no. The Precious Vigilance Committee is the only answer."

This produced a cheer of agreement from the crowd. Slocum had to admit that killing everyone aboard a stage, just to rob it, was going too far. Either somebody had gotten an itchy trigger finger and had opened fire, or the road agents didn't want to leave any witnesses.

If it was the latter reason, Slocum knew there would be more robberies. The road agents were planning on working the road between Coeur d'Alene and Precious, and they wanted to spend some of their money drinking in those towns without fear of being recognized.

He looked around and wondered if any of the couple dozen men gathered had cold-bloodedly cut down the employees and passengers of the stagecoach line.

"Men, we got a problem," came a booming voice. "I say we need to nip this lawlessness in the bud. We're law-abiding citizens. We must stop these road agents before they get any bolder."

"Yeah, Farnsworth, you ought to know all about stealin'. 'Cept you do it in the courts!" This produced a round of laughter at the lawyer's expense.

"I know who the robber is," Farnsworth said in a low voice. By not shouting, he forced everyone to listen to him. His words strangled the words in any heckler's throat.

"There is only one way to stop such a bandit," Farnsworth went on, "and that's to stretch his neck!"

"Now you quiet down with that, Mr. Farnsworth," came Kent's voice. The marshal pushed through the crowd. "If you have any information on who's responsible for this killin' and robbin', let me know. Not some vigilante."

"I know who it is, Marshal," Farnsworth said. Slocum went cold inside. He knew what was going to be said. Slocum started backing away. He didn't get too far.

"The man responsible for these stagecoach robberies is none other than John Slocum!"

As if Slocum had a signpost pointing at him, all heads in the crowd turned and a hundred eyes fixed on him. Slocum watched helplessly as the crowd turn into a mob.

A lynch mob.

12

Slocum backed off, knowing he wasn't going to get away alive. They would either string him up on Farnsworth's charges or they'd gun him down in the street. There were too many of them to possibly fight. But Slocum intended to take a few with him.

His hand went for his six-shooter but a strong grip caught his wrist and kept him from drawing.

"What's going on here?" bellowed Marshal Kent.

"Him, Marshal, he's a road agent!" came the echoing shout. Slocum recognized Howe's voice.

"Yes, Marshal, do your duty. Arrest him," said Farnsworth, pushing his way through the crowd. "He's a newcomer. Did these terrible killings begin before Slocum came to Precious?"

"Hell, yes, they did, Mr. Farnsworth," said Kent, his mouth screwing up in distaste. "We been plagued by stagecoach robberies for months and months. Slocum's only been in town a couple days."

"He must be the one," Farnsworth insisted.

"I couldn't have killed anyone," Slocum protested. "I just came in from the LuLu Belle. Howe tried to burn us out!"

Slocum saw that his alibi wasn't carrying any weight. Stan Howe wasn't likely to admit to trying to dry-gulch him and burn Lurene in the cabin. And with Farnsworth having the crowd's ear, Slocum felt the hemp tightening around his neck.

"Anyone but Miss Macmillan who can verify that?" asked Kent.

"Howe. He was responsible for burning down our cabin." Slocum twisted free of the marshal's grip, but he didn't move to draw his six-shooter. The crowd circled them. If he tried to throw down now, gunfire from a dozen directions would leave him a bloody, lead-filled corpse ready for the potter's field outside town.

"Slocum, maybe we'd better go to the jail where we can talk this over." Kent shoved Slocum toward the ring of men.

"Are you arresting me?" Slocum demanded. His mind raced. He wasn't going to be locked up in the town jail. He'd be a sitting duck for Farnsworth and Howe. Worse, so would Lurene. She needed him to keep those wolves at bay.

"These stage robberies are getting serious," Kent said, more for the benefit of the crowd than in response to Slocum's question.

Slocum looked around and saw the confusion on the faces around him. Only Farnsworth was intent on stirring up trouble, and Kent had effectively taken away the lawyer's thunder. He pushed Slocum through the crowd and then walked a half step behind. Again, Slocum wondered what he ought to do. The marshal knew about the judge killing back in Georgia, but he hadn't done anything about it.

But what if he had found another wanted poster? One for train or stage robbery? That might change Kent's opinion of the man he was marching off to his jail. And it might just be enough to cool the hotheads in town and assure the marshal of a job.

Slocum fretted but decided while Kent allowed him to keep his Colt, things weren't too far out of hand. Going through the narrow door into the jailhouse gave Slocum a shiver of anticipation, though. Kent had played fair enough with him up till now. But there was no doubt he was beholden to Farnsworth.

"Set yourself down, Slocum," Kent said, pointing to a rickety chair in front of his desk. The marshal went around and dropped heavily into his own chair and hiked his feet to the corner of the desk. Rocked back, he laced his fingers behind his head and stared hard at Slocum.

"What now, Marshal?" Slocum asked.

"That's what I'm tryin' to figure out," Kent said. "You're the kind who'd think real hard about robbing a stage—and then you'd do it. I can see it in your face."

"You read more than most men. All I'm doing in Precious is defending Miss Macmillan's claim."

"Yeah, her brother's claim at the LuLu Belle. That's another matter, Slocum. I don't much care if you lock horns with Farnsworth over a hole in the ground. Somebody's making life hell for me by killing passengers on stages. Even if it's not in my jurisdiction, I get blamed for it all." Kent let out a gusty sigh, then went back to looking hard at Slocum, as if this might break his spirit and make him confess to every crime ever committed in Precious.

"Howe tried to burn us out about the time the robbery was taking place," Slocum declared. "Or was it before sundown when the killing happened?"

"Best I can make out, it was late afternoon."

"The vigilantes were out at the mine. They left just after you did, now that I think on it. Was there time for me to ride to wherever the stage was held up, do the killing, and then get back to town?"

Kent scratched his chin as he thought, then put his fingers behind his head again. "Reckon not, but Farnsworth is intent on gettin' those fine folks outside riled up. Why don't we just set here a spell and let them cool off?"

"Or let him get them all het up for a lynching," Slocum shot back. Kent still hadn't demanded that he pass over his six-shooter. That meant the marshal wasn't likely to arrest him, but time worked against Slocum now. Every second Farnsworth was outside and he sat here was a new nail in his coffin. The lawyer was expert at twisting people around to his way of thinking. He wouldn't have stayed a lawyer if that wasn't true.

Loud noises outside the jail made Slocum whirl around. His hand rested on the ebony butt of his pistol. Phil came bursting through the doorway and planted himself squarely in front of Kent's desk.

"What's all this bullshit about you arrestin' Slocum for the stage robbery and killing?" Phil shouted. "He couldna done it. We was out at his mine when the shooting was going on."

"I was determining that for myself," Kent said, not getting too excited. He glanced past the vigilante and saw a half dozen of Phil's vigilance committee outside. They looked angry that their good work that afternoon was being put in a bad light.

"We ain't gonna let you take him, Marshal."

"What?" Kent's eyes narrowed. He dropped his feet off his desk and stood. Slocum felt the tension rising. The marshal saw his power slipping away and being usurped by the vigilance committee. Slocum wasn't sure Kent was the kind of man who would allow that.

"You heard me," Phil said, rubbing his hands on his corduroy pants. "Slocum here ain't guilty, and there's no reason for you to take him. Me and the boys talked it over. It ain't right, so you're gonna let him go."

"I haven't arrested Slocum," the marshal said in a cold voice. "I was just questioning him."

"Then there's no reason why he can't come join us for a friendly drink," Phil said, relaxing a mite. He looked both relieved and triumphant. Slocum knew Phil hadn't backed Kent down, even if he thought he had.

"I don't care if y'all drink yourselves blind," Kent snapped. He glared at Slocum but did nothing to stop him from leaving.

The cold Idaho night surrounded Slocum and cooled him down fast. He hadn't realized how close to breaking into a sweat he had been.

"Much obliged to you and the vigilance committee," Slocum said. "I don't think he was going to arrest me."

"Not with us around," Phil said, puffing up his own importance. "We knowed you was innocent. We were all together when the robbin and killin' happened, or purty damn near together. Unless you could fly, there's no way you could have done the crime. Come on now and buy us a drink."

"Seems reasonable," Slocum said, wishing he could get the hell out of Precious and back to Lurene.

As they walked to the Gold Tooth Saloon, Slocum was thinking hard. He had been toying with the notion that Farnsworth might be behind the stage robberies. Unless he had a passel of men to ride alongside Howe, that didn't look too likely now. The same alibi Slocum had was true for Farnsworth and Howe. They couldn't have raced across the countryside to hold up the stage any more than he could have.

Slocum spent ten dollars buying some of the barkeep's good beer for the vigilantes. It irked him a little, but he considered it money invested rather than spent. He was running low, however, and would either have to find men who didn't know the odds and wanted a game of poker or the LuLu Belle would have to start producing.

As he sipped his beer, Slocum looked around and saw Enoch Carson enter the Gold Tooth and sit down at a corner table. Carson was so intent on getting into a game that he didn't notice Slocum watching him. Slocum watched as the skeletal miner played a careful game of seven card stud. He thought the man might be cheating but couldn't tell without getting closer and watching how he dealt. His hole cards tended to be too good too often, but the other miners in the game didn't seem to put much store in this run of luck.

Slocum shrugged it off. Let the old galoot fleece his sheep. It wasn't his money being lost to a card sharp.

He turned when someone let out a wolf whistle. Glancing over his shoulder toward the doorway, Slocum saw Lurene there motioning urgently to him.

"Gents, I got to leave you," Slocum said. "There might be more trouble out at the mine."

"Sure, Slocum, we understand," Phil said, giving him a broad, knowing wink. Then the vigilante's grin faded, and he said, "If you need our help, let us know. You're one prince of a fine guy."

"Thanks, Phil. I'll do that." Slocum almost choked on the words. Individually, he would probably like most of the men comprising the vigilance committee. Rolled up into one mob, he knew how dangerous they were. He'd rather play with sweating dynamite than cross them. Phil thought too much of his own ability and it would get him—and maybe the others—killed one day soon. Marshal Kent might do it, or Farnsworth could have a hand in it. Even the mysterious band of road agents working along the Precious–Coeur d'Alene road wouldn't have much trouble with this band of amateur lawmen.

"Do they need to whistle and hoot like animals, John?" Lurene asked as he ducked outside. Once more, Slocum was glad to be outdoors. He sucked in a lungful of air before asking Lurene what was troubling her.

"I was getting—lonely all by myself at the mine."

Slocum didn't ask if she was lonely or spooked. He wouldn't have faulted her any if she'd admitted she was frightened. Getting burned up in a fire could put fear into strong men.

"So that's why I was glad to get your message. I came into Precious right away."

Slocum spun and faced her. "What message?"

"Why, I found a note on the buckboard seat. I was up on the hillside sifting through the dirt, looking for the deed when I heard the horse neighing. I went down, and there was your note."

She held out a scrap of paper. Crudely scratched on it in block letters was the simple message: Come on into Precious. The signature was hardly more than an S.

"I didn't leave this," Slocum said. "I've been having words with the marshal."

"And enjoying yourself with your friends," Lurene said, missing the point.

"Someone left this to lure you away from the mine. How long did it take to get into town?"

"Longer than in daylight," Lurene said, frowning. "The road is so rocky and there's not much moonlight tonight."

Slocum glanced up at the stars. High, thin clouds slipped over the moon, making the night darker than before.

"An hour?" he pressed.

"More," Lurene said. "Why would anyone decoy me into Precious? There's nothing at the mine they can hurt. Not after they burned the cabin. With the mine all blasted shut—"

"Squatters' rights," Slocum said. "Maybe Farnsworth wanted you away so he could move in his own squatters. We'd have to run them off if we wanted to prove our claim."

Lurene shook her head. Blond hair spilled out and caught occasional moonbeams, turning to liquid silver. He paused to collect his thoughts. She had a way of distracting him something fierce.

"The vigilance committee knows we are in dispute with Farnsworth. If he tried that, they would back us up. They spent the day out there and they know."

Slocum had to agree. But there had to be some reason for luring Lurene Macmillan into town. He started to mount up when Lurene pointed to the buckboard.

"Let's ride together," she said. "Your horse can follow along, just as it did before."

Slocum wanted to hurry back to the mine, but he wondered if the note wasn't a failed ambush attempt. Perhaps Lurene had found it too soon. The back shooter might have wanted her to leave in the morning and she had foiled his plan. Slocum just didn't know.

He climbed into the buckboard beside her. The wagon rode harder than before, lacking any weight in the bed. The last time he had driven this road, he'd had the small area filled with supplies and Lurene's belongings.

Lurene rested her head on his shoulder as they left town, going back to the LuLu Belle Mine. Before long, Lurene's hand ran down his arm and caressed his thigh. Slocum felt himself responding when Lurene's probing fingers worked lower and found the growing bulge at his crotch.

"This isn't the place," he warned her. "We have to get back."

"John," she said in mock reprimand, "however did you grow up? The horse isn't going to stray from the road, and it's a good hour to the turnoff at this pace."

"What are you suggesting?"

Lurene grinned and spun around on the hard seat, dropping into the narrow bed behind the seat. She took the reins from his hands and fastened them to the side of the seat. Then she opened the front of her dress. Twin mounds of flesh gleamed in the moonlight. Shadows danced here and there and made her appear to be something more than human. An angel. Even more, Slocum thought.

"The horse won't stop," she said. "I don't want you to, either." Lurene dropped to the bed of the wagon and lay flat. Her knees went up and she pulled her skirts around her waist.

Slocum saw she wasn't wearing any of her frilly undergarments. The pale gold hair was turned into spun silver in the moon. She lifted her hips a little and wiggled.

"Come on, John. Let the horse do the work—and we'll have all the fun."

He couldn't turn her down. He slipped off his gun belt and then worked to get his jeans undone. He let out a gasp of relief when he released his long, hard shaft from its cloth prison.

"I need you now, John. Don't worry about anything else." Lurene reached out to him. Slocum dropped to his knees. The bucking wagon jolted and jarred him. He let his weight down on top of Lurene, but he didn't immediately enter her. He bent over and ran his tongue across one bare breast.

The woman shuddered when he reached the crest. He toyed with the nipple he felt hardening more and more there, then darted across to the other breast. Pressing down hard, he felt the frenzied beating of her heart inches away.

Slocum's fingers went under the woman and cupped her buttocks, cushioning them a little from the rough ride.

"I need you so, John. Please," she sobbed out.

He let the motion of the buckboard propel him forward. He almost crushed her as he lost his balance, but he took no notice and slid easily into her. Locked together at the loins, they simply lay there for a moment. Pleasure burned in Slocum's body. The movement of the buckboard produced unexpected lurches and bounces, and this added to his enjoyment. He had to do nothing but stay still and let the motion of the buckboard push their passions to the breaking point.

But he found it impossible to simply lie still. Lurene struggled under him, lifting herself off the wooden bed, driving her groin into his, tensing and relaxing her inner muscles. The pressures mounting within Slocum forced him to begin moving back in response. Slowly at first, then with greater speed and force, he roused their innermost desires.

Lurene shrieked long and loud as waves of passion surged through her. Slocum felt her tightness around him squeeze down even more. She was clutching him in what felt like a velvet-lined vise. Then Lurene lifted herself on her feet and began swaying back and forth while Slocum was still deeply buried inside her.

He couldn't hold back any longer. The woman's beauty, her skill, the moonlight, the motion—it all crashed down on him as he exploded like a stick of buried dynamite.

"Never felt anything like that before," Slocum admitted as he slipped to one side and lay next to the blond. "Never thought of letting the horse go on by itself while I—we—"

"I'm surprised at you, John. This is something I'd've thought you would have tried before."

Slocum didn't answer. He'd never spent much time in a buckboard, much less with a woman. If he went anywhere, it was on horseback.

"Now that I've done it once, I'd like to try it again," he said, stroking her bare breasts with the palm of his hand. His fingers caught up a nipple and crushed it. Then he captured her other breast in the same hand. Lurene sucked in her breath, then let it out in a long, low sigh of pleasure.

"We've got time," she said.

And they did. Just after they'd finished making long, lingering love in the back of the buckboard, they reached the turnoff to the mine. Slocum hitched up his pants and settled his six-shooter in place while Lurene fastened her dress.

Almost primly she sat beside him as he guided the horse up the road to the LuLu Belle. Lurene Macmillan continued to amaze him. She was a wildcat when it came to lovemaking, yet turned almost shy and prim when they were finished. She was wanton and coy at the same time. Slocum had never met anyone quite like her.

"There's the mine," she said. She sniffed deeply, then coughed. "The burned smell is still in the air."

The heavy odor was about all that remained of the cabin. Slocum didn't smell anything else burning, but then, there was little enough remaining. Most of their supplies had gone up in the blaze since Slocum had stored everything in the cabin. Buying more would have to wait until he got some money.

"There's some reason you were lured out of camp," Slocum said.

"Are you sure you didn't leave the message?" Lurene asked. She gripped his arm hard. "I certainly enjoyed the trip back from town with you."

Slocum nodded absently, then jumped from the buckboard and began prowling around. Everything seemed to be as he'd left it, but he had the feeling he was missing something. He searched the ground for signs of intruders and found only small patches of dirt that didn't seem to belong to Lurene or him.

"What did you find?" the blond asked, kneeling beside him.

"Can't rightly say," Slocum admitted. "If someone came through the patch of dirt higher on the hill, it might have stuck to his boots and then scraped off here."

"Why come over the mountain like that?" Lurene asked. "This is more than a hill. It's tall and some of the cliffs are hard going without someone to lower you."

"Maybe somebody just walked through the dirt." Slocum went up the hill to where Lurene had been sifting dirt in her hunt for the baking soda can with Charles Macmillan's deed in it. He found a long, thin boot print that wasn't his. And Lurene's shoes left a different imprint, smaller and narrower.

"He came by here and stopped for a while over here," Lurene said, tracking back on the footprints. "It looks as if he was digging for something. The baking powder can!"

Slocum shook his head. Their intruder hadn't taken something from a hole. He had dug the hole and left something. It looked like a small grave. Slocum used his hands to move aside the loose dirt. A canvas bag had been buried a few inches under the soil.

"What is it, John?" asked Lurene, reaching out to touch it.

"It's a canvas bag," Slocum said grimly. "A U.S. Mail pouch, like they use on stagecoaches."

He ripped it open and went cold inside. Hundreds of letters spilled out, along with a smaller bag containing one hundred dollars in gold coins. The spoils from a stage robbery had been buried where anyone could find it, if they'd been put on the right track.

13

"What is this, John? I don't understand." Lurene Macmillan sat cross-legged beside the shallow hole he had scraped in the ground. She just stared at the canvas mail bag.

"It's one hell of a lot of trouble, for us," Slocum said. He didn't have time to explain her to her. "You watch this for a few minutes. I need to do some scouting."

"What? Where are you going?" Panic rose in Lurene's voice. She reached out to stop him, but Slocum shrugged her off.

"I'll tell you what I think about this when I get back. It won't be too long."

Slocum began backtracking, trying to find where the intruder had come from. The thin boots were easy to follow—up to the edge of the dirt area where Charles Macmillan's cabin had once stood. The logs someone had used as a base to lever the cabin down the slope was about where Slocum lost the trail.

He dropped to his hands and knees and tried as hard as he could to find any spoor. He thought he saw tiny scratches on rock, maybe from a piece of metal, but he couldn't be sure. He kept working backward on this path, then looked up and scratched his head.

Slocum stood and walked briskly around the mountain in the direction of Enoch Carson's cabin. He stopped when he came to the rim overlooking the valley holding the Phantom Mine. He saw that Carson hadn't returned from town yet— or at least there wasn't any smoke coming from the chimney in the cabin.

Slocum considered going down into the miner's camp, then changed his mind. Time weighed down heavily on him. He had realized immediately what the buried mail bag and gold coins meant. He almost ran back to where Lurene still crouched beside the canvas bag. She had spilled out the gold coins and was counting them. She looked up when he stopped at the edge of the dirt.

"There's one hundred dollars here, John. Charles must have buried it. I never realized he had done so well with the LuLu Belle!"

"He didn't," Slocum said. "Did you see that mound of loose dirt earlier when you were looking for the deed?"

"No, but—"

"You would have seen it instantly in broad daylight," Slocum said. "It wasn't all that hard to find in the moon-light."

"I don't understand. If Charles didn't put it there, who did? And why is there a bag of mail with the gold?"

"You don't pull milled and minted gold coins out of the ground. If your brother had buried this, he'd have put nuggets or bags of gold dust into his treasure trove." Slocum began gathering the mail and stuffed it into the canvas bag. "Let's go downhill. I want to dump this in the cabin."

"But it's all burned," Lurene protested.

"Another fire's not going to be noticed there," Slocum said. He lugged the heavy bag down the hill, Lurene trailing after him with the smaller sack of gold coins.

Slocum pushed aside a patch of burned wood and found enough wood to start his own fire. He used a lucifer to get a blaze going again, then fed it carefully with the letters from the mail bag. Lurene looked on silently. Finally, curiosity got the better of her.

"I still don't understand. Where did the mail come from? And why are you burning it?"

"Whoever's been robbing the stages is trying to frame us," Slocum said. "I'd bet my last dollar that this is from this afternoon's robbery." He quickly explained how all the passengers, the driver, and the guard had been murdered.

"That's terrible," Lurene said. "But no one would believe we had anything to do with such a horrible crime."

"This is hard evidence, and Farnsworth tried to get the vigilantes to lynch me as a road agent," Slocum said grimly. He pushed the ashes around, added a few more pieces of wood to the fire, and made sure there wasn't even a stamp left. He sifted through the ashes, sprinkled them over the fire, and then scattered those ashes. It would take more than skill to find any trace of the letters he had burned. It would require a miracle.

Getting rid of the canvas bag took more time. Slocum had to cut it into strips and feed it into the fire an inch at a time. When he had finished, he gave the fire pit one last check. All incriminating evidence was gone.

"Why not just take the canvas bag somewhere and leave it?" asked Lurene. "We could always deny knowing anything about it if it was found along the road. And the people would have gotten their mail."

"You're not thinking right," Slocum accused. "Somebody's trying to get the marshal to arrest us—or the vigilance committee to string us up. They won't hesitate in hanging a woman, if they thought you had anything to do with this afternoon's robbery and murder."

Lurene went pale. She put a hand to her throat and wobbled a little. Slocum didn't have the time to comfort her or to be sure she didn't up and faint on him. He took the sack of coins from her and juggled them in his hand. Slocum was thinking hard what to do with them. Being coins, they weren't as easily identified as the mail. One gold double eagle looked about the same as any other.

He didn't have time to go through and check to see if any of the coins had been specially marked. And Slocum doubted that was necessary. Whoever was trying to get them in dutch with the law wouldn't go to that length. Just mentioning such a special mark would be suspicious, and whoever was going to this trouble was cagey enough to avoid such a trap.

"The well," Slocum said suddenly. "The water's so filthy foul tasting, it won't matter if we hide the coins there."

"But John, I don't want to just throw this away," Lurene protested. "We can use the money. I'm running low on funds."

"So am I, but I'd rather be poor and alive than rich and dangling from a cottonwood." Slocum took the bag of coins and hiked to the well. He found a small limb and tied the drawstrings on the bag to it, then tossed the bag into the well. It seemed to fall forever, then made a distant, tiny splash.

"What's going on?" Lurene asked. "Tell me, John."

"Just keep your mouth shut and don't admit to anything," Slocum said. His nose wrinkled at the stench coming from the well. Something was down there contaminating the water. But he didn't have time to think on it. He heard the pounding of hooves.

It hadn't taken long for whomever was trying to frame them to rattle the right cages.

Kent, a deputy, and two vigilantes Slocum recognized as having been in the Gold Tooth drinking his beer reined back a few yards away. The marshal dismounted, reached for his six-shooter, and motioned for the other three to dismount, also.

"What can I do for you, Marshal?"

"You know damned well why I'm here, Slocum." The edge to Kent's voice told Slocum that someone had poured a real story into the lawman's ear. He was fuming mad, feeling betrayed by a man he thought he was helping out of a tough spot.

"Well, Marshal, *I* don't know. Why are you here?" asked Lurene. She shot an angry look at Slocum, then turned back to the lawman.

Slocum hoped she remembered his words about not revealing anything. If she did, there'd be dead men all over the hillside. And he didn't intend to be one of them.

"I got a note sayin' you had some of the loot from this afternoon's stage robbery buried around here somewhere."

"Who gave you the note, Marshal?" Slocum asked. He knew the answer but wanted Kent to spit it out in front of his deputy and the two vigilantes.

"Can't say. It wasn't signed. But I got enough evidence to come on out here and search the place." Kent waved to the three men who fanned out and began searching. In the moonlight their search was more effective than it would have been at new moon, but they couldn't be sure they weren't missing anything until sunup.

"I reckon Farnsworth had something to do with you coming right on out," Slocum said. Kent stood with his hand resting on the butt of his six-shooter, ready to cut Slocum down at the first sign of resistance.

"He's been doin' some more agitatin'," Kent admitted. "But the vigilance committee is getting on my nerves. All the time now, they're lookin' over my shoulder. I had to come out."

"And something in you believed that note? Really, Marshal Kent," chided Lurene. "I am surprised at your gullibility."

"I have to follow any lead I can, ma'am," he said lamely. Kent cleared his throat and called, "What are you findin' up there?"

"A lot of muck, Marshal," came the answer rolling down the hill. Two of the men rooted through the soft dirt where the cabin had been. The deputy worked on the cabin's ashes. Slocum was glad he had done such a thorough job. In the dark, they'd find no trace of the U.S. Mail bag, its contents, or the gold he'd tossed down the well.

"If you thought I'd really held up the stage, you'd've thrown me in jail when you had the chance," Slocum said. "Has something changed?"

"Damned vigilantes," muttered Kent. Louder, he said, "I've been looking through the wanted posters, Slocum, and your face hasn't come up. One of the vigilantes thought he recognized you, but I think he's been doing too much boozing."

Slocum let out a tiny sigh. Marv must have shown his old poster to Kent. He had done well getting a look at it, but this showed how high the town's emotions were running. Any picture, no matter how faded or unlikely, was being shown around as the culprit holding up their stagecoaches.

"Marshal," said the deputy, looking like a lump of animated coal, "I can't find nothin' in that mess. The whole damn cabin's been burned down. He mighta done it to hide something, but if'n he did, I'll never find what's under it all. I burnt myself on some embers that are still smoldering."

"We reported how Mr. Farnsworth did this," Lurene said primly. For the world, she sounded like a schoolmarm. "He tried to burn us out. Or more likely, that horrid Mr. Howe did."

"Slocum mentioned the fire," Kent said, holding his anger in check by sheer force of will. To the deputy he said, "You didn't find anything? Nothing at all?"

The deputy shook his head sadly and tried to rub some of the soot off his hands. All he did was get his pants dirtier than they had been before.

The two vigilantes came down the hill, in hardly any better condition. One spoke up. "Marshal Kent, we been all through there. Somebody's been diggin' up a storm, but there's no sign of a mail bag or gold or much of anything."

"What are you hunting for?" Kent demanded.

"Gold, Marshal, gold," said Slocum. "There's no telling where it might be found."

"Go to hell, Slocum," snarled Kent. "Let's get out of here, men."

"Sorry you made the ride out from town for nothing," Slocum said insincerely.

"You button that smart lip of yours, Slocum. I've got my eye on you. You might think you're bein' savvy, but you'll slip up one of these days." Kent spun and stalked to his horse. He mounted and rode off, his deputy at his side.

The vigilantes rode over and looked down at Slocum. "We're with you, Slocum. We're beginnin' to think the best thing we can do is run that rascal Farnsworth out of town on a rail. He's behind this, ain't he?"

"He might be behind a lot of the woes you're trying to change," Slocum said.

The two vigilantes wheeled their horses and rode after the marshal, taking it easier as they went.

Slocum didn't pay them any mind. He worried about Kent. The man wasn't anybody's fool, and he was getting backed into a corner. When a smart man felt he couldn't go anywhere, he got downright mean. If something didn't change quick, Slocum knew he was going to have to shoot it out with the marshal.

14

The explosion rocked the mountain. A rough brown tongue of dust and rock licked out of the LuLu Belle and brought a rain of sharp pebbles down on Slocum's head. He ducked but still felt the stabbing sting as he endured a dozen cuts. Coughing, he poked his head up and looked at the mouth of the mine.

"Did you open it, John?" came Lurene's voice through the dusty haze. "I can't tell."

"I can't, either," Slocum admitted. He pulled up his bandanna and pushed through the new fall of debris from the mine. Stopping a few feet away, he looked at the rock he'd blown free. He wanted to be sure all the dynamite had detonated. A powder monkey in a mine counted the explosions to know if some sticks didn't go off. Slocum hadn't been able to tell since his had detonated simultaneously.

He approached cautiously. From what he could tell, the dynamite was all blown. What was left looked like decent ore, but he couldn't tell without doing some work on it. Hefting a chunk of rock the size of his fist, Slocum held it up and studied the veins running through it. A slow smile crossed his face.

"What is it, John? Did you hit it big?" Lurene came up and peered at the rock in his hand. For all she knew he might have a solid gold nugget or nothing but worthless bedrock.

"I'd say this is a good vein. Your brother must have missed it."

"He might have followed a better vein into the hill," suggested Lurene. She refused to admit her brother didn't know enough about mining to make a decent living at it. From all Slocum had seen of the LuLu Belle before it was brought down around his ears, Charles Macmillan was a fair miner. Nothing special, just fair.

Slocum wondered if he could squeeze even more show metal from the mountain. He wiped sweat from his forehead, smarting as the salt burned his head wound. Each time he touched his forehead was a reminder of getting bushwhacked. Slocum had more to do here than pull gold from the chary rock.

"Who's coming up the road?" Slocum asked. He looked around to where he had put his Colt Navy. He fetched it, checked the loads in the chambers, then tucked the six-shooter into his belt. There wasn't time to strap on his cross-draw holster.

"Hey, Slocum, howdy. How's the minin' coming?" shouted Phil. Slocum waved to the vigilante, wondering what brought the man back. If he had ridden out to the LuLu Belle at the head of a posse, it would have meant more trouble. Slocum glanced toward the well with its gold coins, then back to the mounted man.

"Doing all right," Slocum allowed. "What brings you out here from Precious? Don't have any more road agents to catch?"

"Hell, we ain't caught a one of those snakes," Phil admitted. He leaned forward and wiped his forehead with his bandanna.

Slocum almost duplicated the gesture but held back. His head felt as if it would break apart at any minute, the burning along his forehead almost more than he could stand.

"I'd offer you some water, but something's polluted the well," Slocum said. "We've been hauling water up from down yonder." Slocum pointed to a spring down near the main road.

"That's all right. Thought you might like to know a thing or two I overheard in town." Phil spat. "You been a square shooter with us, Slocum. Least I can do is let you know the circuit judge from over Idaho City way is coming to Precious tomorrow. You might want to put your claim in front of him."

"What kind of man is he, this judge?"

"Fair. Hard, but fair. Never heard no complaints about him bein' bought. Leastwise, there's no way Farnsworth could afford him."

"Thanks," Slocum called. "This will be a big help."

"You can buy me a shot and a beer next time you're in town," said Phil. He turned and put his heels to the horse's flanks. Slocum watched him vanish down the road.

"This is good news, John," bubbled Lurene. "We can go to this judge, and he'll guarantee our claim!"

"Reckon that's the way it seems," Slocum said. He mistrusted Phil. Why would the man come all the way out here to tell him about the judge? They weren't friends. The best he had ever done was buy the man a few drinks. Slocum shrugged off his suspicions. He naturally mistrusted vigilantes.

"What do we do?"

"I've got some pay dirt for the assayer," Slocum said, pointing to a pile of ore he had mucked from the mine. "That'll establish there's something here. And I've been meaning to find the surveyor and find if he ever laid out this claim for your brother."

"With the men in town who remember Charles, this is all we'll need." Lurene did a little dance of joy. Slocum wished it was as easy as she thought. Farnsworth was a slick devil and knew how to jump a claim legally. The check Slocum had made of the land records showed most of them missing. In some Coeur d'Alene court, the clerk had said.

Destroyed, was what Slocum thought. Without solid proof in the form of the deed Charles Macmillan had hidden, there would be the devil to pay getting a judge to give them a solid claim.

Slocum sat on the pile of ore and started thinking. He might be approaching this from the wrong angle.

"John, do we go into town now?" asked Lurene.

"There's no sign of the deed your brother hid?" he asked, knowing she would have told him if she'd unearthed it.

"No, none. I wish I'd paid more attention to how he hid it."

"I wish I could figure why someone moved his cabin from up there," Slocum said, looking uphill.

"That's not important now. We have so much work to do. We'll be in complete ownership by the time that judge leaves Precious."

Lurene went to get her meager belongings together for the trip to town. Slocum went over the ore samples, getting the best. Then he sat and used his knife to scrape off pieces of gold from others. He dug into the rock and transferred the scrapings into the cuts he made. Salting the claim wasn't legal, but Slocum wasn't out to win the marshal's approval. He had other plans.

By the time Lurene brought the buckboard around, Slocum had his ore ready for assay. He dumped it into the rear, wishing he'd saved just one gold coin from the stagecoach robbery. That would have pushed the assay well past the level he wanted.

They rode into town, Slocum pensive and Lurene chattering constantly about how her brother was going to be vindicated. Slocum came out of his preoccupation when he saw the hubbub around the stage depot.

"Looks like another stage has been held up," Slocum guessed. He worried that they might try to pin this robbery on him, too. "Go on and get a room at Mrs. Addington's, if you can," he told Lurene.

"What will you do for a place to stay?" she asked.

"There's always a place to stretch out." He saw her shock at the notion he'd spend four bits simply to lie down on a saloon floor overnight, as so many miners did. "Don't worry. It's only for the night. After we talk to the judge, we'll be able to afford the best Precious has to offer."

"I won't simply sit and wait, John," she said. "We're talking about bringing my brother's killers to justice."

"Talk to as many of the store owners as you can. Get them to agree to tell the judge they knew your brother was working a claim of his own. If you can find any IOUs, that'll help. Agree to pay them off—if we get clear title to the LuLu Belle."

"That sounds like bribery," Lurene said uneasily.

"Call it what you will. The mine's legally your brother's. So are the debts. It only seems fair to pay what he owed, with what he worked so hard to prove." The logic made Lurene nod.

"I'll see what I can do. Where are you going?"

"I'll be at the assayer's office," he said. "And I want to talk with the county surveyor." Slocum kept looking at the growing crowd around the depot. Lucas came out and started shouting. It looked like a play being run onstage over and over.

Slocum dropped from the buckboard and tethered his Appaloosa to a rail, then walked to the depot.

"Another one. And the driver and *two* guards were killed," raged Lucas. "You're not doing a damned thing, Kent. You got to *do* something to stop this!"

"You know the problems," Kent said. He looked around the crowd, his eyes lighting on Slocum. Slocum's green eyes met his gaze and held it. He wasn't guilty; he wasn't backing down. Kent broke off and went back to listening to Lucas's complaints.

"Call out the cavalry. You need men to patrol that road. Use those vigilantes! Do *something*!" Lucas's voice was strident. At the edge of the crowd, Phil moved forward.

"We're volunteering to ride along with every shipment out of Precious," the vigilante said. "If we have to send a dozen men, we'll do it."

"There's no need to—"

"Kent here ain't gonna do nothing," Phil went on. "So we will!"

A cheer went up. And through it cut Farnsworth's sharp voice. "I told you who was responsible. You don't need to guard the shipments. Just arrest the ones responsible."

Farnsworth glared at Slocum, and again the vigilante came to Slocum's aid.

"I was out at the LuLu Belle talkin' with Slocum about the time the stage was held up," said Phil. "He ain't responsible, so quit tryin' to say he is."

Slocum nodded in Phil's direction in way of thanks, but his thoughts turned in other directions. Phil was Slocum's alibi. It worked the other way. Slocum was Phil's, too. It always seemed that the vigilante was conveniently near when the stage was being stuck up. Slocum didn't think the vigilante was responsible, but he might know more about the robberies than he let on.

There were many ways to get rich in a boomtown. The hardest way was pulling gold out of hard rock ore. The easiest was taking the gold after someone else broke his back digging it from the ground.

Slocum saw the crowd was beginning to disperse. Lucas continued his angry harangue, Marshal Kent the unwilling audience. Phil and Farnsworth stood and argued. Slocum went directly to the assay office and found the elder Klarner knocking a sample from a crucible. The man looked up from his work.

"Thinking of getting some more ore assayed?" Klarner asked.

"Got it here. I'd appreciate a rush on it, even if your boy's the one doing the work. He seems competent enough at assay."

"I trained him myself," Klarner said, trying not to smile too much at the compliment given his son. "Might be able to get to this right away. Been slow lately. Too many holding back shipping gold, so the ore's building up and who cares what's in it until they're ready to smelt?"

"Thanks," Slocum said. "Can you tell me where the surveyor's office is?"

"Blind Jess?" Klarner laughed. "That's what we call him around here. He's got an office a couple streets over and upstairs over the bank."

"Thanks."

Slocum went out and found the brick bank building. A window on the second floor carried the simple words, J. Smith, Surveyor. Slocum found the side stairs and went up. The door stood open to give some ventilation to the hot room.

A man hunched over a drafting table, a map stretched out in front of him.

"You, uh, Jess Smith?" Slocum asked. He hesitated calling the man Blind Jess, although the man's thick glasses made the name less than a slander.

"Surely am. What do you need, young fella?"

Slocum told him about the LuLu Belle and Charles Macmillan's claim. Smith took off his glasses, wiped them on his shirttail, then nodded sagely.

"I remember the claim. I laid out the plat myself. Lemme see. Where is it, where is it?" Smith went to a stuffed file drawer and pawed through the haphazard maps there. He pulled out a large sheet and dropped it on top of the map he was studying.

"See this? That's the Macmillan claim." Smith's gnarled finger traced out a line around the LuLu Belle.

"What mine is that?" Slocum asked, pointing to the large one that seemed to surround Charles Macmillan's.

"The Phantom Mine. That surly son of a bitch Carson owns it. You know, he tried to do me out of my surveyor's fee? Tightfisted old vulture."

"So you can testify that this is Charles Macmillan's claim?"

"I can testify I was paid for him and these were the boundaries. Whether he recorded it over at the land office is another matter."

"Thanks," Slocum said. He'd have a fight on his hands, but Blind Jess Smith seemed a good witness to have in his corner. In spite of his worry about the man's competence, the surveyor proved better than most at his job.

Slocum got halfway down the exterior staircase when he stopped. Coming up was Stanton Howe.

"I got business with you, Slocum." Howe widened his stance. Slocum wondered if this was where it would end.

He turned slightly so his gun hand was free. It would have been better if he could have faced Howe on level ground. Here he was caught between a brick wall and a six-foot fall over a wooden railing.

"Speak your piece," Slocum said.

"The boss wants to see you. Mr. Farnsworth's over at his office."

"In Coeur d'Alene?"

"Don't be smart. He's got an office across the street. He seen you goin' up to the surveyor's. He wants you in his office *now*."

"I don't have anything to say to him."

"Mr. Farnsworth don't take a brush-off easy, Slocum," warned Howe.

Slocum thought hard on the matter. It might be that Farnsworth wanted to smoke a peace pipe. Slocum hadn't made any secret what he was doing around town. The more people in Precious who knew he was establishing Charles Macmillan's—and Lurene's—claim to the LuLu Belle, the better. Farnsworth might have seen the light and was willing to settle.

"Is it about the mine?" Slocum asked.

"He don't confide in me. Not things like that."

Slocum went down the stairs and stopped next to Stanton Howe. He sniffed deeply.

"What are you doing?" asked Howe, angry at Slocum's sniffing.

"Your clothes need airing. They still carry the stench of a burning cabin," Slocum said. He pushed past Howe and walked across the street. He saw Farnsworth look up from a desk inside. The broad window provided the lawyer a good view of anyone going to the surveyor's office or into the bank.

Slocum paused for a moment, the hair rising on the back of his neck. He looked over his shoulder and saw that Howe had vanished. His back was safe, at least for the moment.

Slocum went to the lawyer's office door and paused. Farnsworth looked at him, his face drawn and pale.

"You wanted to talk to me?" asked Slocum.

"Yeah, Slocum, I do. Come on in. Sit here." Farnsworth stood and motioned to a chair at the far side of the desk.

Both Slocum and Farnsworth heard the back door creaking open at the same time. Farnsworth half turned, then shouted, "No!"

Slocum drew and fired a second too late. Farnsworth fell forward, hit his desk, and slid to the floor. Slocum started to shoot a second time at the back shooter at the rear door, but the man had vanished. He started for the rear door to chase down the killer.

Then all hell broke loose.

15

"You shot him!" came the cry from the door behind Slocum. "You killed the lawyer!"

Slocum spun and pointed his smoking six-shooter at the man in the door. The man turned pale and backed off, holding his hands in front of him as if this might hold back any bullet Slocum sought to bury in his gut.

"The killer was out back," Slocum said. "He shot Farnsworth from the alley and then hightailed it."

"Whatever you say," the frightened man said. He was as white as a sheet and shaking hard. He kept backing until he got to the middle of the street, then he turned and ran off screaming for help. Slocum considered plugging him, just for the hell of it, just to shut him up. But the ruckus was already drawing too much attention. Men drifted from the saloons to see what was wrong.

And from the far end of the street, Slocum saw Marshal Kent striding along, a shotgun balanced in the crook of his left arm. The man was loaded for bear and ready to tangle with his weight in wildcats.

Slocum shoved his pistol back into its holster, then knelt beside the lawyer. Farnsworth's eyes were open but weren't looking at anything—and never would again. Slocum reached over and lowered the man's eyelids. He hadn't liked him when he was alive, and now Slocum liked the lawyer even less. By going and getting himself killed like this, he put the blame squarely on Slocum's shoulders.

"If I'd wanted you dead, I'd have done it face-to-face." Slocum growled at the dead lawyer. He rolled him to his side and saw where the bullet had entered Farnsworth's back. The slug had ripped into important bones and probably tore apart his heart.

"Damned good shooting, finding his black heart," Slocum said. He looked up and saw a small crowd gathering across the street. Men pointed and Kent came up to talk to the man who had seen Slocum in the lawyer's office.

It wouldn't be long before they were all hot on his trail, both the law and the vigilance committee. Slocum didn't kid himself about Phil having any real friendship for him. They'd shared a drink or two and there it ended. Phil saw being a vigilante as the way to becoming important in Precious.

Slocum rummaged through the papers on Farnsworth's desk, hoping for some clue why the lawyer had wanted to speak to him. He found nothing of any interest. And time had run out for him. The marshal and a half dozen armed men were crossing the street. Slocum wasn't sure the marshal had seen him until he went to the back door.

"Slocum, dammit, stop or we'll shoot!" The marshal hefted his shotgun and leveled it. At this range, Slocum wasn't worried about it. He ducked out into the alley just as the marshal cut loose. The entire front of the lawyer's office was peppered with buckshot. Slocum heard the plate glass window shatter and a collective gasp go up from the crowd surrounding the marshal.

Kent was serious about stopping him, even if he didn't stand much of a chance with his scattergun at this range. Slocum ran down the alley, hoping to head off the crowd. It wouldn't take but a few minutes before the vigilance committee caught wind of a murder and wanted a piece of his hide.

Slocum skidded to a halt at the end of the alley and looked up and down the adjoining street. He knew he was crazy thinking he might see the man who had gunned down Farnsworth just standing there, waiting for who knew what. The street was almost empty, the few people along it working at their businesses. He didn't have time to stop and ask any of them if they'd seen anyone running from the alley a few minutes earlier.

"Slocum, stop!" came the angry shout from behind him. Slocum walked quickly along the boardwalk, trying not to draw too much attention. He ducked into a saloon, then went out a side door, curving back to the street between Farnsworth's office and the bank.

A few people milled around, talking about the marshal going after a cold-blooded killer. Slocum kept to the shadows the best he could, found his Appaloosa, and mounted. He rode down an alley, away from the lawyer's office.

Precious was going to be too hot for him in a few minutes. He had to make the best use of time he could.

"Howe," he muttered to himself. "Howe would be the one to find." Farnsworth's hired gun could tell the marshal it had been Farnsworth who had called Slocum to his office. That didn't prove that Slocum hadn't got all fired up and shot the lawyer in the back, but it was a start. With some luck, he could explain that the single shot fired from his six shooter had been aimed at Farnsworth's murderer, not at Farnsworth. But he'd have to get the chance to explain.

Then Slocum went cold inside. He didn't know where Stanton Howe had gone. The gunman might have had it in for his boss. Farnsworth might not have had anything to say. Howe might have set it up to shoot Farnsworth and frame Slocum.

Slocum pushed this out of his mind. It didn't fit the facts. Howe hadn't been nervous or anything other than his usual angry self. There wasn't any indication he was doing more than delivering a message Farnsworth had given him.

"Howe," he repeated. That was a place to start, but Slocum didn't think it would take him too far. Howe wouldn't be inclined to talk, no matter what. Either he had tried to frame Slocum or he was out a good-paying job.

Slocum ducked down low as he rode past the Gold Tooth Saloon. He saw Phil, Marv, and several other vigilantes inside drinking. They might recognize his horse, and he didn't want them noticing him and calling out for him to join them. Any delay now meant a tighter noose around his neck.

Slocum put his heels to the Appaloosa's flanks and galloped to the edge of town. Mrs. Addington's Boardinghouse came into view. Slocum heaved a sigh of relief when he saw Lurene's buckboard out back. She had been able to get her room back.

He hit the ground running and jerked the Appaloosa into the barn. Slocum dropped a chain across the mouth of the stall to keep the horse inside and ran to the back porch. Out of breath, he knocked on the door.

"Yes?" an elderly woman asked. She held the door tightly, as if he might push past her.

"I need to speak with Miss Macmillan. It's important."

"Yes, well, I suppose." The woman fought with her sense of propriety, then said, "Wait here. Whom shall I say is calling?"

"Slocum. She knows me." Slocum looked toward town, expecting to see the marshal and a hundred men hell-bent for a lynching on his trail. He tried to keep himself calm. They might not string him up right away. That judge was coming to town tomorrow on his way back to Idaho City. They might let him live to stand trial.

Then they'd hang him from the nearest cottonwood tree.

"John, what's wrong?" Lurene came out. Slocum looked over her shoulder, into the house. He didn't want to say anything that would get Lurene into trouble. If the old woman was the owner of the boardinghouse, she probably had big ears.

"I have the supplies you sent me for, ma'am," Slocum said. Lurene's eyes widened. She started to protest, then realized what he was doing.

"Oh, yes. Let me check them before I pay you."

"They're out back. Near the barn," he said, turning so Lurene could pass by him even as he hid his face from the older woman still watching. It wouldn't do if she got too good a look and the marshal came asking questions. He saw shadows moving back in the house and knew Mrs. Addington was satisfied enough for the moment to allow Lurene outside with this stranger. The thought that the woman didn't know what he and Lurene had done in her bathtub struck him as suddenly funny.

"Why are you laughing, John?" asked Lurene. "I don't understand what's going on."

"I don't have time to explain," he said, pushing everything from his mind but the predicament he was in. "Lurene, listen carefully since I don't have time to repeat it."

"Why? Are you in trouble?"

Slocum saw that he had to give the woman a complete explanation or she would be in more danger than ever. He quickly told her how he had been lured into Farnsworth's office and the events that occurred afterward.

"This is terrible. We need to go to Marshal Kent and explain.

He's a reasonable man. I'm sure he will understand."

"Yeah, sure," Slocum said sarcastically. The bitterness was lost on the woman. She saw everything in terms of truth and lies, right and wrong. It never came to her mind that Slocum could be innocent and still get convicted of a crime.

"That's no way—"

"Listen hard," Slocum said, interrupting her. He felt the noose tightening even more. "I have samples being assayed at Klarner's. He's the only assayer in town. Jess Smith is a surveyor and has records of your brother's claim."

"Wonderful! Then we can—"

Slocum motioned her to silence. "That doesn't prove Charles ever registered the claim. With Farnsworth dead now, there might not be anyone contesting clear title to the LuLu Belle. You'll have to go to the judge yourself and present your evidence."

"But where are you going? I promised you half the claim. You can't run off and let them think you're a killer!" Lurene was incensed at such behavior. Slocum didn't bother telling her he was a killer, and any judge would take one look at him and know it.

"We'll let this business with Farnsworth blow over and see about settling up," Slocum said. "I won't go far, but I do have to go."

Slocum started to say something else, but it eluded him. He worried over it, because it had been important. Somehow, an important clue to the puzzle of who killed Farnsworth had come and gone faster than lightning. He tried to shake it off and believe the thought would return to him. He started to go.

"John, wait." Lurene rushed to him and kissed him hard. He pushed her away. There wasn't time. Now or maybe ever.

"See the judge, but don't mention my name. Give him all the evidence you can from Klarner's assay and Smith's maps. And get the others to testify, if you need them, the shopkeepers and the rest." He looked at Lurene Macmillan for what might be the last time.

She was distraught but as lovely as ever. Her blond hair floated in disarray as a soft, warm breeze blew past her oval face. Her skin was soft and white and he remembered the curves of her body against his, the passion they had shared, everything about her.

He swung into the saddle and looked for the best route away from Precious. Taking the road was suicidal. The vigilantes would have patrols along it by now. And going back into town was even worse. The marshal would have spread the word about what a back shooter John Slocum was. He might even have told the town about Slocum's judge killing back in Georgia, though Slocum doubted this. Kent would have to explain why he hadn't arrested a judge killer as soon as he found out.

Riding slowly, he made his way across the countryside, working his way up the elevation toward a high road above Precious. The stones turned under his horse's hooves, and the going got steeper. Soon enough, Slocum had to dismount and lead the Appaloosa up the slope. Precious sat in the valley spread out below him.

As Slocum caught his breath after the hard climb, he tried to see any sign of pursuit. He couldn't be sure they were after him, but he spotted a half dozen tight knots of riders along the main road, on both sides of town. Precious buzzed with activity. The miners were getting out of their glory holes and coming to drink what scant profits they'd made.

"All of them will know Farnsworth's dead and who the marshal thinks is responsible." Slocum wasn't sure he'd ever be able to return to Precious.

And there was little reason for him to want to. Lurene

Macmillan was all that had kept him here for even a handful of days. Slocum considered robbing one of the stages as it made its way along the road from Coeur d'Alene or from Precious. He had started out considering how best to rob the stagecoach. With only a few greenbacks wadded up in his pocket to show for his trouble, he ought to consider ways of riding out a mite richer than he was.

He remembered the gold he'd tossed down Charles Macmillan's well. The branch he had tied onto the bag would likely give some flotation to it, but the bag would rot after a spell and dump the golden contents to the bottom of the water. Still, climbing down into the well would be safer than sticking up a stage.

Slocum swung his horse around and headed back up the slope. He saw the high road a few yards away. It might as well have been a mile for all the progress he made. The shoulder of the road was too steep for him. Slocum began leading his Appaloosa parallel to the road, edging upward.

He slipped and slid but kept moving until he was almost up to the road. Some sixth sense made him pause.

"Quiet, old fella," he said, reaching over and putting his hand over the Appaloosa's nose. The horse tried to nicker, but Slocum silenced him. Something was wrong, and he didn't know what it was.

Slocum held the reins down with a rock and finished the climb to the roadbed. He dropped flat when he saw the riders approaching.

Marshal Kent led a posse of more than twenty men! And Slocum had blundered squarely into them.

16

Slocum fell flat on his belly as the posse rode toward him. He wanted to slither like a snake and get back over the edge, but he didn't dare move. It was almost twilight, and they might miss him if he didn't draw any attention to himself.

But he worried about his horse. The animal was standing just a few yards below him barely able to keep its footing on the loose stone. If the Appaloosa made any noise, the marshal and the men with him would have a brand-new prisoner for the town jail.

Slocum watched as Marshal Kent led the posse past him. Hooves flashed just inches from his face. He lay still, not daring to move. The last horse passed by after what seemed an eternity. To the riders, he might have been nothing more than a log alongside the road or a strangely shaped rock. Slocum let out a lungful of air he hadn't even known he was holding as he rolled back over the verge.

"We got to make tracks," he told his horse, patting the Appaloosa's neck in way of thanks for not betraying him. The horse pawed at the gravel and almost slipped. Slocum knew he'd have to get off the mountainside quickly or they'd both go tumbling back into Precious. And after a fall like that, it wouldn't matter who saw him.

Slocum struggled to get the huge horse onto the road, then faced a dilemma. If he rode behind the posse, he might be seen. And he wasn't sure where the road led. If he turned and went back down the hill, he was positive the road went directly into Precious's main street. That wasn't a good idea, even with the lawman out scouring the countryside for him. The vigilance committee would have worked up everyone in town to be on the lookout for him by now.

Not having much choice, Slocum mounted and rode slowly after the posse. He kept an eye peeled for an ambush. He had no idea why Kent was taking this road. Slocum had chosen it almost by accident, so maybe Kent had done the same.

"Howe," Slocum kept repeating. "I've got to find him. Who wanted Farnsworth dead?" There were too many questions and not enough ways open for him to answer them.

In spite of his attention, Slocum had drifted too much into thought about finding Howe. He rounded a bend and came upon three men in the road. Two carried rifles, and the third was unmounted and struggling with his horse, which reared and pawed the air.

"Havin' trouble?" Slocum called, startled but knowing he couldn't run or fight. All that was left to him was bluff.

"My horse pulled up lame," said the man fighting to keep control of his horse. He quieted the horse and grabbed the bridle with strong hands. The horse still shied away but wasn't fighting as hard now. "Think it's just got a rock under the shoe."

"Want some help?" Slocum offered.

"Thank you muchly. I do appreciate it. These two yahoos won't do anything but laugh." The man indicated the two men with rifles.

Slocum dismounted and kept his Appaloosa between him and the armed men. The miner fighting with his horse grabbed hold with both hands to keep the horse from rearing again. Slocum lifted the horse's leg and used his thick-bladed knife to pry out a rock that was wedged under the edge of the horse's shoe. He released the hoof and stepped back quickly. The horse was still skittish but controllable now.

"Thanks, mister," the man said. "You with the posse?"

Slocum hesitated, not knowing how to answer. That the men hadn't recognized him was a bit of luck. Pushing it much farther wasn't too smart.

"I was looking for Marshal Kent. They told me he came this way," Slocum said, not answering the question directly.

"He's on down the road. He and some deputies are thinkin' on setting a trap for that back shooter."

"What's one less lawyer?" Slocum asked, knowing how dangerous a game he played.

"That's so. Especially a low-down, no-account serpent like Farnsworth. But nobody ought to get shot in the back."

"A lot of that's been happening in Precious," Slocum said. "Remember Kenny Moore a few days back?"

"Right after that Slocum fellow came to town, too. I say, we string him up and we done ended a string of cowardly murders." The man climbed back into the saddle. Slocum saw that the horse limped a little and needed a good smithy to reset the loose shoe, but he wouldn't pull up lame for a spell.

"You look to be doing fine now," Slocum said. "You say the marshal is somewhere ahead?"

"Reckon so," the miner said. "You might take that there trail and go up and over the mountain. It's a shortcut."

"Where you going?" Slocum asked.

"We got to patrol this road," another of the posse chimed in. "You're welcome to ride along with us."

Slocum balanced the dangers he faced. He came to a quick decision. "Don't mind if I do. Getting over the mountain on a rocky path in the dark doesn't look to be anything I want to try. I was on my way out to some of the claims to the east of town."

"I hadn't heard anyone was being sent that way," the miner Slocum had helped said.

"Phil's getting everything under control," Slocum said. "He's not happy with the way the marshal's handling this."

"I know he's got a burr under his saddle about the marshal," the miner said, "but Kent's a decent enough sort."

"There've been a whale of a lot of stagecoach robberies," Slocum said, eyes darting around for a way off the road. He knew continuing would only bring him to the rest of Kent's posse. The trail over the top of the mountain might get him ahead of the lawmen, but he didn't see that as a good idea. Riding behind the posse was safer, for the time being.

"There's been more gold shipments. Shiny metal brings out the worst in men. Does me," the miner said, laughing.

"Where's that go?" Slocum asked, pointing to a meandering trail leading down the side of the mountain. They had ridden almost two miles in the dark, and Slocum wasn't exactly sure where he was.

"There? Either of you know?" the miner called to his companions.

"Yeah, that goes on down to Enoch Carson's claim. He built his cabin down in the coulee."

Slocum felt something niggling at the edge of his mind. Then he asked, "How's he get his ore to the stamping mill on *that* road? It's nothing but a path for a horse, and not a good one at that."

"Never thought on it. Old Carson has always had about the best claim in these parts. The Phantom Mine must be about the richest in the Bitterroot Mountains."

The other two vigilantes agreed. One added, "I wish mine was half as good. Old Enoch's tapped into a motherlode. You should see the gold he flashes around town."

"He might have a better road out the other end of the coulee," Slocum said, his mind racing with the possibilities for escape opening to him.

"Could be, though the nearest stamping mill in that direction is forty miles off. Carson's a strange old coot. Secretive. Never much liked him, even if he keeps to himself and doesn't go around bothering folks."

"I'd better go see if he's all right," Slocum said, turning his Appaloosa down the trail. "You men keep on patrollin' along the road. Good luck."

"Same to you, mister," the miner said. He turned and started arguing with the other two men in the small watch along the road. Slocum vanished down the road to Carson's mine, glad to be away from the three vigilantes. They hadn't recognized him, and his bluff had carried him through a tight spot. Slocum knew he would have been caught eventually if he had kept riding with the men. When they joined Kent's posse, someone would have identified him.

He pushed his Appaloosa as hard as the horse could take the winding, narrow, uneven path. Slocum liked the idea that Carson took his ore out the other end of the shallow valley where he had his cabin. The high mountain holding the Phantom Mine—and, on the far side, the LuLu Belle— kept pursuit from town at a minimum. He might be able to reach some other town and just vanish from sight. Leaving Lurene like this bothered him, but his own neck counted for more than the woman's feelings or her brother's mine.

Slocum wished he could have helped her secure clear title to the LuLu Belle Mine, but he had done all that was possible.

With Farnsworth gone, Lurene didn't have any opposition in getting the Idaho City judge to rule in her favor.

"There, there, easy, old fella," Slocum cautioned as the horse began slipping. He hadn't realized he was urging the horse to ever greater speed. He reined back and let the Appaloosa find its own pace.

Slocum also realized he had given up on finding Stanton Howe and clearing himself. He was turning tail and running.

This rankled.

"What choice do I have?" Slocum muttered. His horse snorted in answer, but Slocum couldn't tell which way the Appaloosa argued. Slocum wasn't used to running like a coward, but he might not get away scot-free if he faced the murder charges. Whoever had done the actual killing had him boxed in a perfect frame.

He reached the bottom of the coulee and saw the shallow, sloping grassy sides working their way up to the mountains, which rose in almost sheer cliffs. Slocum dismounted and looked at the path he had come down. If Carson used this way for anything more than a single horse, Slocum found no trace. There was considerable coming and going, from all the spoor he found, but no indication of a wagon loaded with gold ore.

Slocum kept walking, crossing the grassy area and going up toward Carson's cabin. Once again, the miner wasn't home. Slocum began to wonder if Carson lived somewhere else. For someone with what the other miners called the richest claim in the area, Enoch Carson didn't do much hard work.

Poking around, Slocum looked for any sign of digging near Carson's cabin. The grass was untouched, even by deep ruts from a wagon. Slocum did find some indication of cut grass, as if Carson had battled getting something heavy down from higher on the mountain, but it didn't look to be anything from the Phantom Mine.

On impulse, Slocum went to the cabin and ducked inside. He knelt beside the second stove and looked at the legs. The grooves in the feet were filled with soil.

"Dirt. That son of a bitch dragged the stove down from the other side of the mountain." Slocum stood and compared this stove with the fancy wrought iron one hooked up to a vent pipe at the other end of the cabin.

What had been bothering him for days snapped into sharp focus. Enoch Carson had stolen Charles Macmillan's stove and brought it to his expensively decorated cabin.

Every time Slocum had entered Macmillan's cabin, he had noticed the vent hole in the roof but had never asked himself what had become of the stove. Carson had taken it. And Slocum guessed Carson might have been responsible for tipping the cabin off its foundation and causing it to slide down the hillside next to the LuLu Belle Mine. That way, Carson wouldn't have as far to drag the heavy stove.

"You cheat at cards and steal dead men's stoves. What else do you do, old man?" Slocum wondered aloud.

Before he could search the cabin thoroughly for proof that Carson was responsible for killing Charles Macmillan, Slocum heard echoes outside. He stuck his head out the cabin door and heard horses coming from the direction he had intended taking.

He rushed out, grabbed the Appaloosa's reins, and jumped into the saddle. Bent low, he trotted the horse up a narrow trail to the mouth of the Phantom Mine. Trapping himself in the mine wasn't smart, but he had nowhere else to run. As Slocum led his horse into the mouth, he saw a half dozen men riding down the valley toward Carson's cabin.

He got only a couple yards into the mine before the clearance dropped. Slocum remembered his earlier foray into the mine and how low the mine's back was. The Appaloosa began getting nervous at the tight spaces and Slocum turned the horse so it could look out into the valley and not get spooked.

"You find anybody?" came the loud voice from down the mountain. Slocum slipped his six-shooter from its holster. They must have found his trail and tracked him here.

"Nobody here. What about up at the mine?"

"Let's go check."

Slocum dropped to one knee and waited. He'd have to fight his way out when the posse reached the mouth of the mine.

17

"I won't be a minute," came the shout. "Carson might be working his claim."

Slocum cocked his Colt Navy and waited for a face to appear in front of him. He intended for his first shot to be deadly. The rest would be more luck than skill, he knew. But one vigilante would be dead, and he might have a chance at shooting his way free.

"Aw, come on. Carson's not working at this time of night. Do you hear him jacking in the mine?"

"No, and I don't see a light," the vigilante said. "I should check, though."

"Go to hell," another called. "We got to patrol this whole damned valley. We don't have time to look into every hole in the rock we find."

"There might be a gold nugget or two laying around inside the Phantom," another said. "Carson never lacks for money. I've seen him lose a hundred dollars on a single hand of poker. The Phantom Mine must be drilling right through the motherlode."

"I'm leaving. Carson's not there, and you won't find bags of gold sittin' in that there mine, either. I been minin' the

Bitterroot Mountains for years and haven't taken out more 'n a couple pounds of gold."

Slocum's heart beat faster as he heard footsteps approaching. Sweat burned into the groove along his forehead and made him aware of everything around him. Mine timbers creaked under the load of supporting the mountain. A faint whiff of gas from deeper in the mine warned of a possible explosion. And a tiny cascade of rocks signaled that Slocum's presence was about to be exposed.

He lifted the six-shooter and aimed where he figured a head would appear. But nobody came into his sights. After a minute, Slocum relaxed a mite. Then he stood, straightening his cramped legs. Worrying that he was walking into a trap, Slocum edged forward.

Dark shapes of riders near Carson's cabin headed toward the road Slocum had come down. He tried to count them and failed, but there was no reason for any of the posse to remain behind.

The cool night breeze dried the sweat on his face and body. Slocum returned his six-shooter to its holster and leaned against the cold rock beside the mine's mouth. Lady Luck had blessed him once again, saving his life—and others.

Slocum had no argument with most of the vigilantes. He knew why they sought him, even if they were dead wrong. And he also knew if they found him he would end up dead. Arguing his point wouldn't do much good. Even if he got his day in court, the evidence against him was overwhelming. Unless he took the law into his own hands, he'd be destined to swing.

Slocum waited a few minutes before leading his Appaloosa from the mine. The horse snorted and tried to rear. Slocum held the horse down and gentled him until the Appaloosa stood silently. Trying to figure out what to do, Slocum felt an increasing weight of despair. The high road was being patrolled. And so was this valley.

"You can bet the LuLu Belle is crawling with vigilantes," he said to his Appaloosa. "Where does that leave us?"

Slocum couldn't run, and hiding was getting to be impossible. Farnsworth hadn't been liked by many of the citizens in Precious, but his murder was the final nail in the coffin. There had been too many stagecoach robberies and too many back shootings.

Slocum touched his own wound and felt lucky there hadn't been a third bushwhacking victim.

Slocum knew what was eating at the citizens of Precious. The boomtown was a dangerous place without road agents lurking behind every rock along the way. Many of the miners died in accidents. Their work hours were long, and few got more than a few dollars' worth of pay dirt out of their claims in any day.

Even worse, the best mines were owned by the bigger companies from San Francisco and Seattle and back East. They paid three dollars a day for a twelve-hour shift. These might be the luckiest of the miners in the Bitterroot Mountains. They were paid no matter how little—or how much—gold they teased from the unyielding earth every day.

Coming after Slocum gave them a sense of doing something indisputably good for the town, and it relieved the boredom all miners felt. They were ill-housed and poorly fed, had little to do but get drunk and chase after the few whores in Precious, and then return to the mines in the morning for more work. A necktie party would be talked about for months.

"Can't run, don't want to stay here," Slocum said, thinking out loud. "That leaves only one place to go, no matter how dangerous it might be now." He swung into the saddle and rode the Appaloosa around the mountain, going toward the LuLu

Belle Mine. When he got close to Charles Macmillan's claim, he cut away, heading straight down the side of the mountain until he found a deep, narrow ravine that still trickled with spring runoff.

In an hour Slocum was back in Precious.

Like a magnet pulling an iron needle, Slocum rode toward Mrs. Addington's Boardinghouse. He wanted to see Lurene again but knew better than to ask after the woman. Any gossip would be on Mrs. Addington's tongue, and she wouldn't hesitate calling on whatever vigilantes remained in Precious.

There might be a small chance Slocum could go from window to window until he found Lurene's bedroom, but he didn't want to take the risk. One mistake and it was over for him. He rode into the barn, dismounted, and took care of his horse. The faithful animal had kept him alive, responding when he needed speed and being quiet when he had to avoid the posse.

Slocum stretched his cramped muscles after giving the horse a good rubdown, then dropped into the empty stall next to the Appaloosa. Within minutes, he was soundly asleep.

Slocum came immediately alert when he heard voices outside the barn. He sat up, hand on his six-gun, then realized it was Mrs. Addington going about her morning chores. The sun was up over the mountain peaks, and he had slept for hours.

He quickly saddled his horse and chanced a quick look outside. Mrs. Addington was returning to her kitchen, an egg basket swinging from her left arm. She was getting ready to fix breakfast for her boarders. Slocum's mouth watered at the smell of baking bread already coming from the kitchen, but he knew it'd be a spell before he had a chance to sit down to a good meal.

Just a few yards away Lurene Macmillan was sitting down to eat, and Slocum wanted to see the pretty blond woman again. He knew that wouldn't be possible until he found Howe and got to the murderer responsible for gunning down Farnsworth.

Slocum rode down alleys and back streets through Precious, getting near the city hall. More and more people were coming out to go about their business. Slocum tethered his horse and walked toward the large, spired building with its fire lookout. A side door stood invitingly open. Slocum slipped through into the cool darkness.

A clerk bustled around, getting chairs placed in neat rows. A large man with a florid face harumped and spat into a cuspidor while he pawed through a stack of papers. He wore a felt hat and string tie, and on the desk in front of him lay an old black powder Remington six-shooter.

"When's this circus going to start?" the corpulent man barked.

"Any time, Your Honor," the clerk said.

Slocum saw a small closet to one side of the room and dodged into it when the clerk came over to shut and lock the side door. Like it or not, Slocum was going to be a spectator when the judge began his deliberations. He gingerly reached out and felt the walls, seeing that he was in a two-foot-square closet filled with odds and ends.

He pushed some of the debris aside and crouched down to peer through the keyhole. The view he got of the room was too limited. With the closet becoming increasingly stuffy, Slocum chanced opening the door a crack. This let him breathe more easily and gave a good view of the judge on the bench.

"Don't have any more time to waste. I want to be home for a good dinner cooked by the wife before sundown," the judge said. He accurately spat and hit his brass cuspidor. "Get those varmints in here so I can make my rulings."

The clerk opened the front doors and people began trickling in. Slocum almost called out when he saw Lurene walk in, head held proudly. She carried a sheaf of papers and a small bag that swung as if it had an ounce or two of gold in it. Slocum smiled. He had salted the ore he had given Klarner for assay.

In Precious, news of such rich ore would get around fast.

"Who's first?" the judge bellowed.

"Your Honor, I have a case to put before the court," Lurene said, her voice just a little shaky.

"Get on with it. Order!" the judge roared. He grabbed the six-shooter and used the butt to rap sharply on the desk. "Be quiet or I'll throw the lot of you into the calaboose."

He nodded to Lurene, who began her story. She finished, saying, "I have everything but the actual deed. Those pages are gone from the land clerk's register."

"And your brother's back East and can't tell you where his deed is?" asked the judge, his attitude softer toward Lurene than the gallery with its whispering men looking for a few minutes of entertainment.

"There are any number of townspeople who will testify they know my brother has been working the LuLu Belle."

"I've seen the records in this city," the judge said, "and unless there is some objection, I'm going to—"

"Wait!" Enoch Carson stormed into the room. "I object. My lawyer got himself killed."

"Your lawyer? What's a lawyer got to do with this?"

"I was negotiating to buy the LuLu Belle from Farnsworth. I paid him good money for the mine, in good faith." The skeletal miner pushed through the crowd and stood before the judge. "By rights, that's my mine, not hers."

"You have any documents attesting to this?" The judge looked at Carson with a skeptical gaze that didn't shake the scrawny miner's confidence one bit.

"Farnsworth had everything."

"Do you know anything about this, young lady?"

"No, Your Honor."

"Then it's open and shut," the judge said. Lurene stiffened as he rapped the butt of his pistol on the desk. And Slocum reached for his Colt. The judge looked to be in Carson's hip pocket. He was shocked to even see the miner in the court. He had no idea Carson and Farnsworth had been dickering over the LuLu Belle.

Slocum peered out into the crowd and started when he saw Stanton Howe pressed into the far corner. He had to take the risk and get to the man. Slocum froze when the judge rapped sharply with the butt of his pistol and cleared his throat to get attention.

"I see for Miss Macmillan's brother. What was his name?"

"Charles Macmillan," Lurene supplied.

"The mine is yours, and I instruct the court clerk to prepare duplicate papers to that effect."

"No, you can't do this!" protested Carson.

"I can and just did. Another peep out of you, and I'll toss your skinny butt into jail. Call the next case."

There was shuffling of people in the court and this gave Slocum the chance to slip out of the closet, unlock the side door, and exit the building. He was still in a heap of trouble, but Lurene had her clear title to the LuLu Belle Mine. He hurried around to the front of the town hall, then caught himself before bulling out into the street. Men rode patrol now, vigilantes intent on finding him.

Slocum tucked his chin to his chest and pulled his hat down to keep from being identified. The vigilantes passed by, but Slocum didn't ease up. They wanted his neck in a noose, and he couldn't forget it.

He swung around and bent double when Lurene came out, chatting with two other women. She was obviously pleased with the judge's ruling. Slocum longed to congratulate her, but he had other fish to fry. After Lurene had gone down the street in the direction of her boardinghouse, Slocum began his search again for Stanton Howe.

Finding the man and getting some information on Farnsworth's enemies from him was the only way he saw of clearing himself. He didn't much care if he shared Lurene's newfound fortune, but he didn't need more wanted posters dogging his heels.

Slocum passed a few saloons but didn't see Howe. On impulse, Slocum headed for the stables a few hundred yards down the street. Set back a ways, the livery doors were open. Slocum saw Howe inside, saddling his horse as he got ready to leave Precious.

A quick glance assured Slocum he wasn't likely to be seen. He hurried to the stable, closed the door behind him, and went over to Howe.

"I'll pay you when I get back," Howe said, mistaking him for the hostler.

"You'll pay up now," Slocum said.

Howe spun, hand going for his six-shooter. Slocum swung hard and hit Howe squarely on the chin. The man's head jerked back, and he fell heavily into the stall beside his horse. Slocum rubbed his knuckles, hoping he hadn't broken any bones.

"Where were you going so fast?" Slocum asked, hand resting on his Colt Navy.

"You got it all wrong, Slocum," Howe said, shaking his head and holding his chin. "I wasn't going to testify ag'in you. I'm getting out of Precious for good."

"I gathered as much," Slocum said. "Tell me about Farnsworth."

"What do you want to know?" Howe's eyes darted around, hunting for any way out of his dilemma.

"Who were his enemies? Who was most likely to shoot the son of a bitch in the back?"

"Everybody in this town. Can't say I knew anybody who loved him."

"You didn't have a grudge against him, did you?"

"No! I wasn't the one who plugged him. After I saw you was headin' over, I went to get a drink. Ask anybody over at the Lone Star. I was there until I heard the gunshots."

"Shots? You heard more than one?"

"Two."

"Then you can tell the marshal. I shot at the killer a split second after he drilled Farnsworth in the back."

"Yeah, sure, I can do that. Anything you want, I'll tell Kent."

"What's got you so spooked?" Slocum asked. "And what can you tell me about Farnsworth being Enoch Carson's lawyer? He came bulling his way into the court saying he had bought the LuLu Belle from Farnsworth. The judge didn't buy into that tall tale." Slocum watched Howe carefully. The man's leathery face paled slightly at the mention of Carson's name, but Howe quickly covered.

"Farnsworth didn't tell me what he was doing. I didn't know hardly any of his clients."

Slocum knew the man was lying through his teeth. Something about Enoch Carson was at the bottom of all his troubles, and he had to put it together. Carson cheated at cards and had stolen Charles Macmillan's stove. Slocum was certain of that. What other deviltry was Carson up to?

A noise outside distracted Slocum for a split second. He saw the wind had caught the stable door and swung it open to reveal an empty street. He whirled back, hand flashing to his Colt.

Howe struggled to draw his six-shooter. He had it out and pulled back the hammer. That was as far as he got before Slocum's six-gun exploded.

The bullet ripped dead center through Howe's chest. The expression on the man's face combined shock and fear. Then he sank to the straw and lay unmoving. Slocum didn't have to examine Howe to know the man was dead.

His only chance for clearing his name had just died, and Slocum had as many questions now as before he'd found Stanton Howe. But he knew where to find the answers.

18

Slocum turned to leave and saw a dark silhouette in the stable doorway. He lifted his six-shooter, ready to blast his way out of town. Whoever stood in the door hadn't been there a few seconds earlier. The door swinging open in the wind was what had distracted him and given Howe the chance to die, but no one had been there then.

"John?" came a voice he knew well. "What's going on?"

"Lurene, I've got to leave Precious now." Slocum relaxed a mite and put his six-gun away.

"But John, it's all working out wonderfully. Look!" Lurene reached into her small purse and pulled out a thick wad of greenbacks. "I sold the LuLu Belle!"

"What?" This startled Slocum. He cast a quick glance in Howe's direction, then stepped forward so Lurene wouldn't see the man's body. There was no need complicating an already complex situation. "Who bought it from you?"

"Mr. Carson. He said, although he had paid Farnsworth a large sum of money, that he was willing to pay even more for the LuLu Belle. So I sold it!"

"He accepted your signature on the deed?"

"Of course. Why shouldn't he?" Again Lurene's naïveté

astounded Slocum. Women couldn't own real estate. And the judge hadn't declared Lurene the mine's owner. He had only upheld her brother's claim. They had been lying, saying Charles Macmillan was back East, hoping to draw out the men who had killed him. Only the murderers would know Macmillan wasn't back East.

There was only one reason Carson would have offered Lurene money—her and not her brother—and Lurene missed this obvious proof of what had happened to Charles. Carson knew her brother would never be able to sign over the mine.

"Here is your half, John." Lurene began counting out the money. Slocum tried to estimate how much Carson had paid. It was a princely sum, but Slocum stopped the woman as she worked through the sheaf of bills. He reached out and cupped her hands.

"Keep it," Slocum said.

"You've gone to so much trouble for me, John. And—" She looked at him with her intensely blue eyes. He didn't want her saying more. A murder charge hung over him that wasn't likely to be erased. And when the marshal discovered Howe's body, there might be a second murder charge added, though that had been a fair contest and Slocum had acted in self-defense.

Slocum kissed her gently, then pushed her away. Lurene resisted and started to speak again.

"You were leaving Precious, weren't you?" he asked.

"There's nothing for me here. Charles is gone. I don't think there is any way we will ever find out who was responsible for his death, or where his body might have been hidden." Tears began forming, but Slocum wasn't sure if it was the loss of her brother that affected her most. What Slocum did wasn't easy for him, either.

"You've got to go back to Saint Louis and make a new life for yourself. The money will give you a good start." He saw the lovely blond on the arm of some rich banker or a railroad magnate. That was her destiny, not riding with him.

"The stage leaves in a few hours. I wanted to sell the buckboard and horse." She chewed at her lower lip, as if screwing up her courage to ask what Slocum sought to avoid. He wasn't any good for her, and she belonged in a world alien to his. Even if she got used to riding the range with him, dodging wanted posters and bounty hunters was no fit life for Lurene Macmillan.

"I'll take care of it. Consider that my pay."

"I do wish we had found what happened to Charles," she said.

"Lurene," he said solemnly, "I'll take care of that, also. I promise that his killer won't profit by his death."

"You know who killed him? It *was* that terrible man Howe, wasn't it? He and Farnsworth!"

"Go on now," he said, gently pushing her from the stable. "Get a good meal, buy your ticket, and go back East."

"I'll never forget you, John."

"I hope not," Slocum said, smiling crookedly. He gave her a last kiss, this one more passionate than before. Then she turned and hurried off. Slocum watched her and knew someone important was leaving his life.

He mounted his Appaloosa and weaved his way through the streets of Precious for the last time, avoiding larger groups of armed men and worrying that one of the vigilantes might see him and raise a hue and cry. Only when he reached the road leading to the LuLu Belle did he breathe a little easier.

The posse couldn't keep the entire valley sealed forever. Putting food on the table would eventually drive the miners back to work after the thrill of the hunt wore off. Their resolve would flag, and he would be able to escape. Reaching Charles Macmillan's old claim showed that they were already relaxing their efforts to find him. He saw where a half dozen men had camped briefly, then left. Marshal Kent might keep chasing him, but Slocum knew he could avoid a single lawman, even with a handful of deputies riding at his side.

Slocum got to the mouth of the LuLu Belle Mine and looked around. He remembered with some longing the night he had spent with Lurene in the cabin, but other things distracted him now. He went to the well and peered down. He lit a lucifer and dropped it. The light vanished halfway to the water. From the bottom rose a faint stench confirming what Slocum had come to suspect was the water's worst pollutant.

He mounted and rode his Appaloosa around the mountain in the direction of Enoch Carson's Phantom Mine. It took Slocum longer than he anticipated, but the delay proved worthwhile. As he rounded the mountain and looked down into the shallow valley holding Carson's cabin, he saw a horse grazing contentedly.

At last Carson had returned to his cabin.

Slocum dismounted and checked his Colt Navy, making sure there was a fresh load in every cylinder. He wasn't taking any chances now. The slightest slip meant he'd end up like Charles Macmillan, and nobody would be wiser.

From the direction of the cabin came loud cursing and the sounds of someone throwing things about. Slocum left his horse and walked on silent feet to the window. He chanced a quick look inside.

Carson had two stacks of paper on the floor in front of him. He pulled letters from a mail bag and added more to the larger stack than he put on a tiny pile of greenbacks.

The door stood slightly ajar. Slocum braced himself, kicked hard at the door sending it smashing into the wall, and pointed his six-shooter straight at Enoch Carson. The thin, tall man grabbed for a Spencer rifle on the floor beside him. He froze when he saw Slocum had the drop on him.

"Afternoon," Slocum said. "Nice day to count the money you got from stagecoach robbing, isn't it?"

"You got it all wrong, Slocum. I was just—"

"That's a U.S. Mail sack. And those letters don't have your name anywhere on them. And I reckon that might be the strong box from the last stage robbery." Slocum indicated a heavy iron box sitting to one side. The padlock had been broken open, but the lid was still closed.

"What are you going to do about this?" Carson asked.

"I need to figure out what's been going on," Slocum said. "And I think I know just about all of it. That mine of yours is a worthless hole in the ground, isn't it?"

"Not worthless," Carson said, chuckling. "Serves my purpose real good. People think I got the richest claim in all the Bitterroot Mountains."

"You rob the stage, then pass it off as gold you mined."

"Nobody ever asks how I pull smelted, minted gold coins out of the ground. Not a one of them fools." Carson's gaze drifted once more to the rifle. Slocum kept the road agent in his sights.

"You're turning real mean. You didn't have to kill everyone on the last couple stages you robbed." Slocum didn't expect an answer and didn't get one. "But there was a reason, wasn't there? You didn't want witnesses so you could bury a few dollars in gold and a stolen mail sack to frame me and Lurene Macmillan."

"Didn't work, damn it. I didn't think you'd find the loot before Kent got out from town." Carson rubbed sweaty palms on his pants. He was still thinking about the rifle, but not as hard now that Slocum hadn't opened up on him. The feral gleam in the road agent's eyes told Slocum Carson would start making offers real soon.

"You killed Charles Macmillan and dumped his body down the well," Slocum said flatly. "You pushed his cabin down the mountain. Why?"

"I thought he had gold buried under it. There wasn't enough worth stealing."

"Except his stove," Slocum said pointing to the second stove in Carson's cabin. "You stole his stove. Why would you go and do a thing like that?"

Carson turned pale. Slocum edged around and opened the door. Stuffed into the stove were enough greenbacks to keep an army warm all winter.

"You couldn't show up with too much paper money, could you? That didn't come out of the mine, so you just squirreled it away." Then Slocum realized how another part of the puzzle fell into place. "You killed Kenny Moore."

"It was an accident," Carson cried.

"Yeah, you thought it was me leaving. You wanted to steal my poker winnings. You're one greedy son of a bitch, Carson."

The fake miner said nothing. He sat near the rifle. Slocum wanted him to go for it so he could have a reason to kill him. Carson was too wary for that. He saw death written on Slocum's face.

"You always gamble with greenbacks and maybe claim to be a big winner. That helps you get some of this into circulation." Slocum tapped the side of the iron stove. It rang hollowly. He couldn't guess how much was inside, but it was probably a thousand dollars. Maybe more.

"We can make a deal, Slocum. You're as crooked as I am. You're a stone killer. I can help you get away from Precious, and give you a good stake to boot."

"You paid Lurene Macmillan with some of this stolen money for the LuLu Belle. You wanted it because you thought I'd struck a new vein of ore. A good mine means you could rob even more stages and look even more prosperous."

"I didn't mean to blow up the mine with you in it like that. It was an accident. You have to believe me."

"I wondered if it was you or Farnsworth responsible for trying to trap me in the LuLu Belle. It didn't much matter, since I've got such a score to settle with you that one attempt more or less don't amount to a hill of beans."

"I'll get you out of Idaho, Slocum, and you can have all the scrip. That stuff's no good to me. I only want the gold. We can be partners, for a while. Look, look what else I can—"

Carson reached inside his shirt. Slocum didn't hesitate. His six-shooter came up, found its target, and discharged. White smoke billowed and Enoch Carson dropped to his knees. He kept trying to get his shirt open. Slocum shot him again, this time through the head. Slocum cocked his pistol and waited a few seconds.

Carson lay facedown on the floor, dead as a doornail.

Slocum went over and rolled the road agent over with the toe of his boot. Carson had half drawn a pepperbox belly gun. It wasn't accurate, but the range had been short, and he might have done real damage if Slocum had faltered for even a heartbeat.

Charles Macmillan, a dozen or more stage passengers and crew, Kenny Moore, and how many others had died at the hands of this greedy, back shooting son of a bitch? Slocum didn't know if it had been Carson or Howe who had tried cutting him down the first time he rode out to the LuLu Belle, and it didn't much matter. Both of them had come to the end they deserved.

Slocum pawed through the stove and pulled out the stacks of

greenbacks Carson had hidden there. Then he searched the rest of the cabin, finding only a few dollars in gold coins. Wherever Carson hid his real wealth would have to remain a mystery. Somebody might come out, another prospector or miner, maybe Marshal Kent or just a traveler passing through, and find it.

Slocum hoped it would be put to good use. He started stuffing the greenbacks into the mail pouch so he could get them outside and put them into his own saddlebags.

After stashing the paper money, Slocum tossed the incriminating canvas sack aside. He had done all he could to bring some peace—and some justice—to Precious, Idaho.

He rode out, wary of any deputies or vigilantes. He saw no one. By late afternoon, he was well away from Precious and far from the reach of even the most aggressive vigilance committee. Slocum paused on a hill. In the distance, he heard the clank and rattle of a team of horses pulling a stagecoach.

He wiped his forehead with his bandanna. The sweat still stung, but the wound was healing nicely. It might leave a scar, but that wouldn't matter much. He'd have something to remind him of Precious and Enoch Carson.

The stage rounded a bend in the road. Two armed guards rode atop it, and next to the driver sat the shotgun guard. They were distrustful of every blind curve and rise in the road, but Slocum knew they didn't have as much to fear now as they had a few short hours before.

He started to wave his hat in their direction, then stopped. Inside the coach he caught sight of Lurene Macmillan. She looked out, her eyes not really seeing any of the countryside.

The stage rattled past, taking Lurene with it. Slocum wished her well, wherever she ended up. He settled his Stetson squarely for the long ride, urged the big Appaloosa down the hillside, and headed west. Seattle might be a good place to spend some of the greenbacks weighing him down.